WHITE OAK PLANTATION

Slavery's Deeper Roots

a novella prequel to

WHITE OAK RIVER:

A STORY OF SLAVERY'S SECRETS

Ora Smith

LIGHTEN PRESS

Copyright © 2021 by Ora Smith

Published by Lighten Press
www.lightenpress.com

Printed in the United States of America

This is a work of fiction.

All rights reserved. No part of this publication can be reproduced, stored in a retrieval system, or transmitted in any form or by any means—for example, electronic, photocopy, recording—without the prior written permission of the publisher. The only exception is brief quotations and printed reviews.

ISBN
978-0-9980410-6-3

Poem and Christmas carol "It Came Upon the Midnight Clear"
by Edmund Sears, 1849

This story is a work of fiction. With the exception of recognized historical figures and events, all characters and events are the product of the author's imagination. Any resemblance to any person, living or dead, is purely coincidental.

Cover design by Lynnette Bonner of Indie Cover Design,
https://www.indiecoverdesign.com
DepositPhotos #13040222 Oak Tree; #140162474 Woman; Envato Elements 50 Flare & Stars Overlays Vol. 1 Sunlight

BISAC Subject Headings
FIC049000	FICTION / African American / General
FIC049010	FICTION / African American / Christian
FIC049040	FICTION / African American / Historical
FIC049020	FICTION / African American / Women
FIC014060	FICTION / Historical / Civil War Era
FIC014000	FICTION / Historical / General
FIC042030	FICTION / Christian / Historical
FIC049060	FICTION / Romance / African American
FIC027050	FICTION / Romance / Historical / General
FIC027360	FICTION / Romance / Historical / American
FIC074000	FICTION / Southern
FIC044000	FICTION / Women
ET020	CULTURAL HERITAGE / African American
TP020	TOPICAL / Black History
TP028	TOPICAL / Christian Interest

Dedication

This book is dedicated to all who wish to join in the reconciliation between descendants of the African enslaved and descendants of American slaveowners. Some of us are one and the same.

And to
my mother, siblings, children, grandchildren, nephews, nieces, and cousins—hoping you will see the family through my eyes and enjoy the experience.

AUTHOR'S NOTE

This story is based on true events of my ancestors. I was drawn to it as a means to discover my own identity. It is not a story of slave beatings or violence, although those horrendous experiences absolutely did happen to enslaved Africans. During my research, while poring through thousands of slave narratives, I read of violence, but I also found stories about life without those evils. While some slaves were not physically abused—and may have been cared for or even loved by their white enslavers—they still never knew freedom. Confusing and emotionally unhealthy on so many levels, the mental turmoil of the enslaved is something we may never comprehend. I did not write this side of history to soften the effects of one person owning another but instead to study the situation on an intimate level. My attempt to tell this story does not diminish in any way the atrocities that occurred because of the Transatlantic slave trade. We cannot rewrite history, and we certainly shouldn't lie about the abhorrent facts. My hope is that in sharing this story we can discuss where those who came before us went wrong and find a way to move forward. Ultimately, now it's up to each of us to decide to do better than our ancestors may have done because when individuals begin to stand up for what's right, that's when the world changes for the good.

CONTENTS

CHAPTER ONE 1
CHAPTER TWO 6
CHAPTER THREE 14
CHAPTER FOUR 16
CHAPTER FIVE 20
CHAPTER SIX 21
CHAPTER SEVEN 24
CHAPTER EIGHT 33
CHAPTER NINE 41
CHAPTER TEN 47
CHAPTER ELEVEN 54
CHAPTER TWELVE 58
CHAPTER THIRTEEN 64
CHAPTER FOURTEEN 69
CHAPTER FIFTEEN 71
CHAPTER SIXTEEN 75
CHAPTER SEVENTEEN 83
CHAPTER EIGHTEEN 91
CHAPTER NINETEEN 96
CHAPTER TWENTY 103
AUTHOR'S HISTORICAL NOTES 113
ACKNOWLEDGEMENTS 118
ALSO BY ORA SMITH 121
ABOUT ORA SMITH...124

CHAPTER ONE

October 2, 1859
White Oak Plantation, Onslow County, North Carolina

Toting two pairs of shoes and an old dress, Spicey crept across the dark landing and down the servants' narrow stairway in her stockings. Betsey, the head houseslave, knowed Spicey's plans to help a runaway slave, but no one else. If Spicey got caught, they'd not whip her, for Massa Gibson not a violent master. The worst be if he sold her away. She couldn't think on such a dreadful notion.

She stopped in the kitchen and found the victuals hidden inside a barrel under a lid. The last couple weeks, Betsey had been leaving them there for Spicey to take to the runaway every few days.

Laying out the old dress on the floor, Spicey put biscuits, smoky smelling ham, and two apples in the center, then rolled it tight. Her heart pounded so hard and loud, she feared the noise give her away. Standing, she pulled the bundle close to her chest, hoping it muffled the thumping of her heart.

Silently, she tiptoed across the new kitchen floor. The door, new too, didn't squeak. Outside, the cool air smelled of woodsmoke and longleaf pine. She hunkered on the back stoop to put on her shoes, keepin' the older ones for her friend, hoping Miss Carrie wouldn't notice them missing.

Once far from the big house, Spicey set out running. She passed the cotton and peanut fields, moving swiftly toward the crick where the pines growed thickest. As she ran, she glanced over her shoulder for anyone following. Ezra, the black slave driver, might be waiting in the shadows for any runaways, and she'd already thunk on what to do iffen he caught her. He was sweet on her. The houseslave Cozy said he might be wantin' to marry Spicey, so if he catches her, she'd just tell him she'd been hopin' he'd find her cuz she be wantin' to know him better.

But really, she prayed he slept at the quarter with the other twenty or so fieldhands. They'd had many long days out in the fields. About now, they should be faraway gone into the world of dreams. Massa didn't have many runaways no-how. Slaves said Massa the best massa they'd ever had.

Hoping Annie Mae hid where Spicey done told her to, she entered a dense thicket and holler-whispered, "I's here." She stopped and stood still, real quiet, listening for an answer.

Annie Mae stepped out of the forest darkness, a smile on her pale, dirty face. Her skin be so light she mayhap mistaken for white. "Ya brung me food, Spicey?" she asked, almost pleading.

"Course I did. Don't I regular like?" Spicey crinkled her brow, feeling a little stung. "Lookee here," she said as she squatted and proudly unrolled her old dress. "I even brung you sumpin' to change into."

Annie Mae let out a little "oh" and touched the linsey-woolsey, running her dirty fingers across a blue stripe. Then she snatched the ham and took a big bite, picking up the other food with her empty hand and putting it into a large apron pocket.

Even though the dress looked old, Spicey was proud of it. She weaved the cloth on the loom. She made the dress with her own hands. She held it up to Annie Mae and figured it should fit, seeing as they were both eighteen and Annie Mae be small like Spicey.

Affer Annie Mae ate, Spicey suggested, "We's need to clean you up some." It wouldn't do for Annie Mae to *look* like a runaway. From her pocket, she pulled out her hairbrush and a little sliver of soap she thunk no one at the big house be missin'. "And see iffen we's can make you toler'ble nuff to pass as white."

Annie Mae's eyes growed big as the silver dollars Spicey once saw stacked on Massa's desk. "I cain't talk as fine as you. Dey know I be a slave."

Spicey afeared Annie Mae right, but affer having thunk long and hard, she wasn't sure what else to do for the girl. "I reckon you could go to po' folk homes and say you do chores for some victuals? Them'll maybe think you's white trash and not ax questions. You then move on affer a day or two."

Annie Mae nodded, but panic lay deep in her eyes. Her face growed paler.

Spicey washed Annie Mae's hair in the crick. Cold and shivery by the time Annie Mae was done bathing, she at least smelled better. She put on her stained underclothes and Spicey's old dress. She tried and tried to squeeze her bare foot into one of the shoes, but it no use. It too small.

She sat on a rock while Spicey brushed her hair. She brushed Miss Carrie's hair every morning and night but brushin' Annie Mae's made her wish they were kin. "You have any sisters, Annie Mae?"

"Naw, not by my mam. My massa is my pappy. He got lil' girls by his new white wifey. Made my mam and brudders and me move outta de big house and into de quarter when he marry her."

The thought bewildered Spicey, so she changed the subject. "What's it like living with a mam?" She snagged a knot in the girl's hair by accident, causing her to whimper. "Scus'm," Spicey said by training and laid her hand on Annie Mae's head, slowly working the brush through the worst of the tangles. Her hair laid long and black like Spicey's but not as wavy.

"My mam . . . she de one dat make me run away." Annie Mae sniffled. "She say she 'member de same look in Massa's eye when he now near me that he had when she young, and I need to skedaddle." She wiped her face.

Her massa her pappy, and he wanna make babies with her? Spicey knowed how babes was made and what Annie Mae said about her massa-pappy made her stomach feel like when she ate a pickled oyster that sat out too long. Because she wanted to help Annie Mae, Spicey didn't think she could share that upset feeling and not hurt the girl's feelings. "I wish ya could live with me. I never seen my pappy. And Mammy die years back. I have no brothers or sisters, no ways."

"'Hap yo massa take me in?"

"Not sure how to ax him that. Who selling you? They will know you's a runaway. My massa stand with the law."

"Ya tole me ya like yar massa and mistress."

"They nice nuff, but they don't see me when I's right there next to 'em. Miss Carrie—my miss—she used to be my friend when we's young'uns, and I pretend she my sister, but she not really." Spicey didn't like admitting the truth a things and chose to talk of something different. "Mayhap iffen you could find life as a white folk, you can live near 'bout and be my friend? We's can be like sisters?"

Turning 'round to face Spicey, Annie Mae shook her head. "Come wid me," she said, her voice getting louder. She gave Spicey a hopeful look with bewitching hazel eyes.

Spicey took the girl's shoulders and twisted her back 'round and started brushing again. What she said made Spicey's breath hitch. "I don't wanna leave the Gibson family. They's not my family, but I have no one else. 'Sides, people will know I's a slave and I git you caught." Spicey stared at her black hands brushing Annie Mae's hair and looked to Annie Mae's white hands on her lap. She'd pass for a white girl by anyone's reckoning. "And what iffen my pappy show-up some day looking for me?" This was always Spicey's hope.

"Yo so clever, ya could pose as my slave and—"

In the distance, hounds barked and bayed.

Annie Mae stiffened. "Oh, Spicey, dey'se lookin' fir me."

Spicey stopped mid-brush, and she looked all around into the darkness of the trees, her insides going cold like she'd drunk straight from the well. "You don't know it's you they'se looking for." Although she tried to sound brave, she had to hold down a whimper. She quickly put the brush in her pocket and snatched the shoes that didn't fit Annie Mae. "I gotta git back to the big house. You run far from here."

Annie Mae stood and turned, taking Spicey in her arms. "I loves ya."

Spicey wanted an affectionate parting, but the dogs barking bested her senses. She pushed Annie Mae away. "Run, Annie Mae. Run!"

Annie Mae ducked into the thickest part of the woods, the brightness of the clean white and blue striped dress standing out among the trees.

Spicey groaned. What had she done? And the hound dogs, they'd smell the reek of ham, making them more anxious for their prize.

Lifting her skirts, she ran toward home as hard and as fast as ever in her life—her prayers sent to God for Annie Mae's escape. "Keep me safe, Mam," she whispered to her dead Mammy's spirit, still turnin' her heart to Mammy when afeared.

The eerie echoes of barking came closer, but by the time she was on the road by the peanut fields, the yapping moved another direction. She slowed her steps, quietly nearing the big house, where she stopped and leaned against a giant old white oak, catching her breath, knowing she couldn't enter Miss Carrie's bedchamber panting. She took the time to close her eyes and pray in earnest for Annie Mae. *Make her feet as wings, Lord.*

The huge, two-story white house of White Oak Plantation glowed in the moonlight. Eight dark chimneys stuck up above the roofline, looking like the bales of hay the fieldhands had made with the new hay press. Gardenia scent held thick in the air. Autumn had been holding off, but it would be on them soon enough, and they'd be moving into town for the winter.

Spicey snuck into the house and up to Miss Carrie's bedchamber, then removed her dress. She tiptoed to the floor pallet where she slept. If Miss Carrie woke, Spicey would say she'd been to the privy. But Miss Carrie never woke, and no one the wiser she'd been meeting with a runaway slave.

Before lying on her pallet, she knelt and said her prayers, pleading with God once again to help Annie Mae get away. She may be the closest hope for Spicey to have a sister—family. Unless, of course, Spicey's pappy returned.

CHAPTER TWO

October 8, 1859
Near Belgrade Road, Onslow County, North Carolina

Caroline Gibson rode beside her father in their buggy.

The air smelled of rain, but none fell. The October afternoon bore a cold, overcast sky with dark clouds so low they appeared to hover just above the trees.

Without warning, tingles ran along her arms, bringing a sensation of imminent tragedy, which she quickly convinced herself was her over dramatic imagination. Reticence, worry, and uncertainty were her weaknesses after all.

She bit her lip. At the moment, she worried over her deepening feelings toward her friend Reverend John Mattocks and whether she'd ever be able to tell him of her affection. She also worried if the new gown she recently ordered would be considered in season. While she'd never mirror any of her beautiful and adept four sisters, she could try to dress as properly.

Thinking of her sisters, she let her mind rest on ten-year-old Sarah. Sick for days, was it she who Caroline should be fretting about? The illness had come on so suddenly.

She scooted closer to Papa.

He held the reigns of a single horse in his hands. A true Southern gentleman, he was always well-manicured and elegantly dressed. Not much taller than her, he was small for a man—with a full mustache, thinning brown hair, and brown eyes.

Mama and all of Caroline's siblings—four sisters and one brother—had brown eyes. Although younger, Hester was almost Caroline's twin in appearance, but Caroline was the only one with unusual green eyes flecked with blue. Papa said they were the color of the waters in the West Indies.

The buggy rounded a bend to a scruffy man in the middle of the road pointing a rifle toward a hedge of tall bushes.

Caroline instinctively reached for Papa, catching the velvet cuff of his overcoat as he brought the horse to a stop about twenty yards back.

The stranger's long hair and untrimmed beard gave him the appearance of a backwoods Appalachian man. He wore a fringed, soiled buckskin coat, gray breeches, and a floppy, sweat-stained hat. Turning a fraction, he tilted his head in disinterested acknowledgment of their arrival, then poked at the tall bushes with his gun. "I know you're in there, girlie. Come on out 'fore I start shootin' at the bushes. Who knows what I might hit?" He spat a stream of chewing tobacco five feet from where he stood.

Were they going to witness a murder? Caroline pushed herself against Papa, clutching his arm.

"What goes on here?" Papa called out.

"This don't concern ya none," the man yelled over his shoulder, keeping his eyes and gun trained on the copse of Mayberry bushes and young willow oaks. *Boom!* He fired the rifle, the explosive blast blowing apart an area of foliage.

Caroline screamed, pushing her face into Papa's shoulder.

His muscles hardened as he fought to restrain the frightened horse.

An involuntary whimper escaped her like a child's lament. Eighteen and too old to cry, she clenched her teeth against the tears.

"Carrie!" Papa shoved her shoulder with his. "Get behind the buggy."

The last thing she wanted was to leave Papa's protection, but she dared not disobey.

He looped the reins around the buggy's iron stanchion, then jumped to the ground.

"Papa, no!" *Don't leave.*

He pointed his index finger at her. "Do as I say."

Papa never carried a gun other than to the Christmas Eve hunt. To approach an angry stranger without a weapon was dangerously foolhardy.

Heart pounding, Caroline willed her legs to move and climbed down from the buggy, stumbling as her slipper caught in her crinolines. She grabbed the metal slats of the carriage bonnet to keep from falling and then pulled her skirts out of the way as she ran to the back of the buggy and crouched. Her legs trembled, threatening to dump her onto the dusty road.

Papa's elegant boots crunched along the rutted road. "Is there someone behind that hedge who has broken the law? We're law-abiding citizens in these parts, and we don't go shooting people *for any reason.*"

"Tain't none of your business, ol' man," the stranger growled. "I'm the law and have ever' right to be huntin' this here mulatto slave."

Caroline relaxed but only a little. A bounty hunter was allowed to track fugitive slaves. She wasn't sure what the law stated about killing them.

The man kept his gun trained on the bushes.

Papa came to his side. "You must be new at this. I doubt her owner would want her dead. Why don't you leave the gun with me and go see if you've wounded or killed her?"

The man's rough chuckle sounded as if he'd never laughed in his life and needed some practice. "How's 'bout ya go see if she's still movin' and drag her out to me?"

To Caroline's surprise, Papa moved toward the bushes, turning his back on the crazy man with the rifle. She grasped the buggy wheel and pulled herself up, sending a whispered plea to God, "Keep Papa safe."

Papa pushed at the thick brush, his progress slow as he climbed through low-growing tangled vines and wild berry bushes. At least his riding gloves would help to clear his path through thorns.

The bounty hunter kept his stance while reloading his gun.

Minutes later, the bushes rattled, and Papa emerged holding the arm of a young white girl who appeared near about Caroline's age. "Is this the girl you're seeking?"

The girl seemed unharmed, pulling against Papa's grasp as he dragged her from the brush. The stripes on her filthy blue and white linsey-woolsey dress were hard to distinguish through grime. Barefoot and obviously of low breeding, twigs stuck out of her tangled, dark hair. At the sight of the man pointing a rifle at her, the girl tried to move behind Papa, but Papa pulled her back to his side.

"That be her. Mighty white, ain't she." He made a noise in his throat which Caroline assumed meant he was proud of himself. "She's been passin' fer white far too long. I been trackin' her fer three weeks. The law says I've ever' right to catch her. Hand her over."

The girl cowered, then sagged against Papa.

"I can't argue with the law." Papa faced him. "Can I see your warrant?"

The bounty hunter shuffled his feet, his face hard and ruddy. "I left it in town with my belongins."

"How do I know this girl's a slave?" Papa asked. "Why'd you shoot at her if you're expected to return her to her master?"

The man's bitter face reddened, and he shrugged.

"I see no reason to put her further in harm's way. She's half-starved and weak. As young as she is, I expect she's a strong worker when well fed." Papa—dressed in fine clothes and much the other man's senior in age, status, and wealth—presented himself as having the upper hand. "I'll take her to Mister Cook, the county marshal," Papa said with determination. "He lives not far from here. The girl will travel with us in the buggy. You can follow. I assume you have a horse somewhere near about?"

The man would be foolish to argue, but it appeared as if he wanted to. "My horse is up yonder 'round the curve in the road." He jerked his head toward the bend. "I'll be travelin' right beside ya, and she ain't goin' no wheres without being bound." He laid his gun across a log and pulled a long, leather strap from his coat pocket.

Papa positioned the girl facing backward toward the stranger, pushing her arms behind her.

"I should beat ya fer makin' me chase ya 'cross two counties." The bounty hunter wrapped the leather strap around both her wrists several times and knotted it. "You're just lucky I ain't have hounds with me. They would'uv done torn ya to shreds."

The girl's legs crumpled, and he yanked her back to her feet by pulling on her bound wrists. She cried out in pain.

"Here now, no need to be rough." Papa took the girl by her upper arm and turned her toward the buggy. "I don't have time for this business." He glanced over his shoulder. "I've a very sick child at home who needs laudanum. I'm on my way to the doctor's now. Mister Cook's home is along the road. I only have time for a brief stop."

The man spat and walked around the bend out of sight.

Caroline came out of her hiding place as Papa neared the buggy, and the mulatto jumped when she saw her.

Papa pulled her by the arm to the opposite side of the buggy and lifted her up.

She smelled of river silt, perspiration, and filth, but Caroline would have never guessed the girl—whose skin was as white as her own—had Negro blood.

The buggy seat was meant for two, but her ill-fed body fit between Caroline and Papa without so much as a pinch.

Moving closer to the buggy's side, Caroline pulled a lavender-scented French lace handkerchief from her mutton-leg sleeve and held it to her nose.

Trembling, the girl stared at the floorboards, but as the buggy started off, she peeked sideways. Dirt caked her long and matted hair.

From a distance, Caroline had thought it brown like her own, but now realized dust made it look lighter than the black that it truly was. She feared there may be lice crawling under the snarled mess and worried the vermin would get on her. She'd tell her lady's maid Spicey to comb kerosene through her hair tonight, perhaps even sprinkle it on her dress before giving it a good washing.

"What's your name, girl?" Papa asked.

"Annie Mae." She cowered.

"Are you as the bounty hunter says, a run-away slave?"

"Yassuh," she quietly answered.

Caroline had hoped for more of an explanation.

"Who's your master?" Papa asked.

"Massa Howard of Duplin Coun'y. Pleeze don' let dat devil man take me back der." Her voice cracked.

"You're owned by Mister Howard. He has the legal right to regain his property."

Annie Mae bowed her head and cried.

Caroline turned her face away, keeping her kerchief to her nose. The girl had no idea who she was talking to. Papa owned over thirty slaves and only once had a slave run. He'd bought that young man in Virginia and owned him a week before he disappeared. Within a few days, a bounty hunter caught the fugitive heading north and brought him back bruised, bleeding, and unable to walk. Papa paid the man but told him he'd never hire him again because of his brutality. Papa believed in keeping his slaves healthy.

Caroline slanted another look at the girl.

Annie Mae needed to wipe her nose, but with her hands bound behind her, she couldn't use her sleeve. "Reckon he don' wan me no mo'," she blubbered.

"Seems if he hired the bounty hunter, he wants you back." Papa slapped the reins, trying to get the horse to move faster. "Where've you been the past few weeks?"

"Doin' dis an dat. Ain't no one know I'z a slave, see'n as I pass." Annie Mae's trembling and tears never stopped.

"I wouldn't have known myself." Papa gave her a side glance. "Do you know what they do with runaway slaves?"

"Yassuh. I'z seen toes and hands cut off and whippin's till they fall down dead. Pleeze don' let 'em do dat to me!"

Caroline shivered and reached for her shawl behind the seat, wrapping herself in it.

They passed the bounty hunter waiting on his horse at the side of the road. He moved-in behind them. Papa asked no more questions. Annie Mae's sobs and sniffles continued.

They reached Mister Cook's home and found him at his stables brushing down a horse.

Papa reined in some distance from Mister Cook and left both girls waiting in the buggy.

The bounty hunter, still carrying his gun, joined the men, and they carried on an unheard conversation. It started to rain and their silhouettes blurred while raindrops tapped softly on the buggy top.

"Why are you so white?" Although hesitant to talk to the slave, Caroline broke their silence.

The girl looked as if she'd stopped breathing. Her light hazel eyes had flecks of gold. Such unusual eyes—almond shaped, exotic, and beautiful.

"My mam light like me," Annie Mae said. "Her hair be kinky though."

The explanation didn't tell Caroline much. "What does your Pa look like?"

The girl glanced toward the men and then whispered, "Mister Howard be my pappy."

Shocked, Caroline didn't know how to respond.

Wind blew heavy rain onto the girls' skirts. Annie Mae shook, and Caroline pulled her shawl tighter. Why would a father keep a daughter as a slave? Have her tracked down by a bounty hunter? Treat her like a criminal? She was the same age as Caroline and, by all appearances, white. Could Caroline somehow help?

Papa stepped to the buggy. Water trailed in rivulets off the brim of his black felt hat, and his breath showed in the air. He scrutinized Annie Mae. "Mister Cook says the bounty hunter has the right to take you back to Duplin County. There's nothing more I can do to ensure your safety."

Annie Mae bowed her head, quaking.

"There are laws governing runaways, and I've done all I can, child. Now that Mister Cook and I know of your situation, the bounty hunter would be foolish to harm you further. You'll need to stay bound, but I'll tie your hands in front so you can hold to the saddle horn."

"Papa, is there nothing more we can do?" Caroline thought fast. "Can you buy her and bring her home?"

"No, Carrie. She's obviously wanted by her owner and not for sale."

"But Papa . . ." Caroline wavered and swallowed hard, searching for another idea. "Might could we . . . maybe take her to Duplin County ourselves?"

"You're being foolish, daughter. You know your sister's ailing at home. We have to be on our way to get that laudanum." Papa pulled Annie Mae's arm to slide her toward him, then lifted her off the buggy.

Her hands were bright red from the bindings, and he untied and brought them in front of her.

"Wait, Papa." Caroline slid across the seat and stepped down, took off her shawl, wrapped it around the girl, and tied the ends to keep it in place. Pulling her bonnet off, she placed it over Annie Mae's matted hair and tied the ribbons under her chin. Spitting rain ruined Caroline's hair ringlets, but she barely noticed.

Head bowed, Annie Mae walked toward the bounty hunter.

Troubled over the future of the white girl who was black, Caroline wondered if she still would've given Annie Mae the shawl and bonnet if the slave's skin had been black. She knew in her heart she would not have.

CHAPTER THREE

October 11, 1859

Days went by. Each time Spicey checked for Annie Mae at their meeting place by the crick, she was never there. Feeling lonelier than before, Spicey ofttimes plopped onto the rock where she'd brushed Annie Mae's hair and cried for a spell.

When Miss Sarah, Miss Carrie's little sister, became sicker, Spicey stayed closer to home, expecting Miss Carrie to want her close. Most every year, slaves and whites got summer sickness on the plantation. But this being October, it took Mistress Gibson by surprise. Spicey had seen Mistress, a wildcraft medicine woman, cure most anything. Like when Spicey ate some black berries she found in the woods. Mistress knowed that Spicey eating crushed charcoal would clear up the fever and racing heart. But no matter what Mistress done for Miss Sarah, she just kept getting sicker and sicker, no-how.

Spicey went into the sick room with a cup of tea from Mistress.

Cozy stood next to the bed, fanning Miss Sarah.

Miss Carrie stood stiff at the window, staring outside at something Spicey couldn't see. Most times Miss Carrie hesitant to act. But this time, she just seemed worried.

"Miss Carrie, Mistress say you try and feed Miss Sarah some tea," Spicey said quietly, not wanting to disturb the reverence that hovered in the room.

Miss Carrie turned and gazed at Spicey as if not understanding her words. Miss Carrie could act a frail thing, but Spicey didn't think she was acting this time. Spicey knowed Miss Carrie wasn't sleeping well cuz they were both up at nights. They'd been praying something fierce. Miss Carrie said she sure God wasn't listening to their words, but she ain't give up yet.

Worryment squeezed Spicey's chest, and she repeated, "Can you help Miss Sarah drink her tea?" Should she give the tea herself?

Miss Carrie came forward like she gonna lay down sick herself but took the cup and saucer. She sat real gentle-like on the bed and stroked her sister's cheek. "Sarah, I have tea for you. Can you sip a little?"

Miss Sarah opened her eyes, and Miss Carrie set the tea on the bedside table while she helped her sister to sitting, then held the cup while she sipped. She swallowed only two times and then laid back down.

A bad feeling seeped deep into Spicey's bosom.

CHAPTER FOUR

October 12, 1859

Caroline perched on the edge of Sarah's bed. The bedchamber smelled of Mama's remedies, a mix of herbal medicines, vinegar and fragrant spices.

"I can't feel my feet." Sarah's voice was hoarse, her throat torn raw by days of violent vomiting.

Leaning over her, Caroline pulled back the quilt.

Mottled hues of veiny blue discolored Sarah's feet.

Chin trembling, Caroline felt the unease of imminent tragedy. This was why she'd experienced the same just days before. It wasn't Annie Mae who would worry her soul, it was Sarah.

Caroline turned away to hide her distress. "Let me rub them for you." She brought Sarah's small foot to her lap, surprised by its coldness. She squeezed her eyes shut and took deep, calming breaths as she massaged. "I miss our games of chess." She tried for a diversion, but Sarah's feeble smile made Caroline feel worse. "Would you like me to open the window?"

Sarah shook her head and closed her eyes. She slept a lot lately. Too much.

Caroline traced long stitches on the Wild Rose quilt they'd made together. Pink flowers and green vines circled an ecru muslin center and worked outward to a darker pink border. Sarah's childlike stitches were large and irregular, typical for a ten-year-old, and she'd hated sewing it. Caroline had kept her sister at the task by asking her questions. It was how Caroline kept chatty Sarah still.

For five days, typhus fever had wreaked violence on Sarah's body. The laudanum Papa and Caroline had brought back wasn't working.

Caroline prayed in her bedchamber each night, begging God to relieve Sarah of her suffering and fever. "Give me the pain," she'd sobbed. "Let my dear sister rest."

Today Sarah rested, but it wasn't the type of rest Caroline had prayed for. Sarah was dying.

Last night, Caroline wrote to John, asking him to pray for Sarah too. His faith was stronger than Caroline's. Maybe God would listen to him more than her?

Moving Sarah's foot under the quilt, Caroline gently lifted out the other, relieved to be doing something helpful, hoping in some small way it gave comfort.

Caroline was Sarah's senior by eight years, but Sarah acted older than her age. Papa had nicknamed her "The Belle of Charm" because of her way with people—so opposite from Caroline. Sarah wasn't a typical little girl who played with ragdolls and spent hours learning sampler stitches. Instead, she visited with family, slaves, or whoever she could engage in conversation and had an uncanny ability to sense what others needed.

Mama entered the bedchamber carrying a tray with a teapot and one empty cup. "How's my sweet girl?" She smiled, but only her lips performed the act. Her eyes held fear.

Sarah briefly opened her eyes, the stare blank.

"She can't feel her feet, Mama. They're very cold," Caroline whispered as if in church.

The teacup rattled on its saucer when Mama placed the tray on the bureau. With a trembling hand, she poured the liquid into the cup. An aroma of huckleberry tea mingled with the other medicinal smells in the room as she brought the cup to the bedside. "Sarah, can you sip some tea?"

"No." The word barely scratched past Sarah's throat.

Mama set the cup on the bedside table and pulled a white kerchief from her apron pocket. She dipped the cloth in the tea and rubbed it across Sarah's lips.

Sarah's tongue peeked from her mouth.

Mama sighed. Her shoulders drooped.

A great sadness settled in Caroline's heart, constricting her chest. Mama was never at a loss to cure. She was known not only in Onslow but in Carteret, Jones, and Craven counties for healing the sick with her concoctions of dried plants, ginger root, and honey—from her own hives, no less. Her healing gift gave credence to people calling her Medicine Woman.

Caroline hoped there was something deeper in Mama's healings. Her beliefs stemmed from a mixture of knowledge of plants and God, combined with her good heart and gentle hands. She had a gift. In that there was power. Caroline always believed in Mama's powers and in her God. If Mama and God couldn't keep Sarah alive, then there was nothing left to believe in.

A groaning sob escaped Caroline's throat.

Mama turned to face her. "Hush, Carrie." Her voice harsh, her gaze slid to the floor, as if making eye contact might burst some kind of dam and spill out her emotions.

Caroline placed Sarah's foot under the quilt and rose. She turned her back and gulped for air.

"Carrie." Sarah's soft voice almost escaped Caroline.

She went to her sister's bedside and grasped her dry, limp hand.

"Will you . . ." She paused and swallowed, every word seeming to take life from her. The Sarah who chattered her days away could barely speak. "Open my door wide . . . and play the piano for me?"

"I would delight in playing for you." Caroline hoped Sarah could hear love in the reply as she leaned down and kissed Sarah's forehead.

When Caroline stepped away, Mama laid herself out on the bed, her large gray skirts billowing over Sarah's small frame, and took Sarah in her arms. "Tell me what *I* can do for you."

Caroline stifled sobs and ran from the room.

The piano gave her a place to express her feelings that she couldn't seem to do with words. In hopes her love for Sarah could be poured into song, she chose John Field's "Nocturne No. 1 in E-flat Major." Lyrically expressive and sometimes gloomy, the song imitated the sounds of nature at night. She should've chosen a piece without such a lonely melody, but it was one of Sarah's favorites.

The music notes unreadable through tears, Caroline played the evocative piece from memory. She emphasized the happier notes that tripped along and reverently played the more subdued ones, imagining Sarah healthy and running and playing games outside with little brother Benny, even though Caroline's heart told her it was not to be. She ended her song, the brilliant chords resonating into a final and tranquil expression of love.

CHAPTER FIVE

October 12, 1859

In the workroom at the loom, Spicey wove osnaburg fabric with a flax warp and jute weft. She'd later sew it into slave petticoats. Not as fine and smooth as Miss Carrie's underthings, but it would do—for it be what Spicey was told would be so.

As she worked, alluring piana music came from the parlor, filling the air 'round her. She wanted to still her fingers, close her eyes, and let the music sooth her worryment about Miss Sarah. But she couldn't rightly be caught dawdling.

The tune embraced life's deepest feelings. All the Gibson womenfolk played the piana, but no one as lovely as Miss Carrie. Spicey never tired of it. The melody filled her soul. Today the song had a reverence to it, as if angels sang from heaven. That thought stopped her in her thinking, and that same deep, sinking feeling as afore came over her.

Suddenly, someone screamed like the Devil run affer her.

Spicey's hand froze with the shuttle in the air. When she caught her breath, she rushed to the large, open main hall foyer and looked up the stairwell.

Moaning came from Miss Sarah's bedchamber.

Miss Carrie came from the parlor and slowly stepped into the foyer. As pale as a haunt, her eyes met Spicey's and pain sat in hers worse than Spicey had ever seen. She ran to catch Miss Carrie in a faint but didn't make it in time. She just missed the door frame going down and laid in a heap of blue chambray fabric with fine lace at the hem. A thought Spicey couldn't account for crossed her mind about how if Miss Carrie got her gown soiled, Spicey have to scrub it out.

CHAPTER SIX

October 14, 1859

While Hester and Benny held Papa's hands and visited with guests, Caroline sat huddled on a chair in a dark corner of the parlor. Her older sisters, Julia and Mary occasionally gave her *the eye* to mind her manners and visit with others. But she couldn't stand there with her siblings. What was she supposed to say as Sarah laid stiff outside the door in the foyer?

The hands of the wall clock permanently set at 3:09—the time her soul had left her body two days before. A thick, black veil draped the mirror across from the clock. The pungent smell of black dye masked aromas from food on the sideboard—brought by neighbors who stood by Mama, touching her, and whispering in dismal tones.

Mama crumpled, hands caught her, and Papa rushed to her as her sobbing grew louder.

Everything in Caroline screamed to escape the suffocation of the room, and she pushed her way past bodies hovering close together with faces all turned toward Mama's grief.

ର୍ଷର୍ଷର୍ଷ

Spicey had made the softest white linen gown for Miss Sarah. Shame to bury it in the ground. But not knowing how these things worked, Spicey hoped it be the dress Miss Sarah greet Jesus in, and that He knowed Spicey made it.

Since no slaves allowed in the foyer or parlor with white folk viewing the body and all, Spicey stood in the front yard with the other slaves. They sang gospel and welcomed the visitors, taking their overcoats and whatnot, while Moses, dressed in black livery, pulled the horses reigns and moved carriages. Too many to fit in the stables, he parked them along the outskirts of the yard. Spicey reckoned the whole county came to give respects.

Fingernails as black as her dress, she hid her hands in the folds of her skirt as she swayed to the singing voices. She'd been at the pots all day yesterday, colorin' all the womenfolk gowns and crepe cloth for the mourning period. The black dye had a nasty odor and smelled up the parlor more than outside where the slaves gathered.

Last night, she try to comfort Miss Carrie, but she wouldn't let Spicey give balm. When she try to pray vocally, Miss Carrie stopped her with a shriek. "There is no God." And done told Spicey to quit her praying or she'd make her sleep on the landing in the cold hall with no fire hearth to keep her warm.

Ezra stepped into the circle of singing slaves, his eyes sheepish-like, glancing Spicey's way. Whenever she caught him looking, her face warmed, and she tried to act as if she didn't notice his attentions. Don't he know she greivin'?

Massa hired Ezra in the West Indies, bringing him here last season. He a big man who carry a whip while in the fields. Spicey never see'd it used but heared the crack now and again. Mistress sensitive to seein' it and Ezra not allowed to tote it near about the house. Massa don't tolerate floggings and all slaves knows he sell 'em easily if they don't behave. Many be orderly just to stay on White Oak. Too many mean massas here 'bouts.

Not many slaves care for Ezra on account he gets special privileges for being a slave driver—the best cabin with a wooden floor closer to the big house, and a horse to use in the fields, and no hard labor. And he a bit uppity and cruel at times. At harvest, slaves worked from "day clean to first dark" as usual, but then Ezra lit lanterns in the cotton house and kept the men at work till the clock struck twelve. Night hours for fieldhands are supposed to be they own, to spend with family and rest their weary bones. Ezra carried no respect for such.

Swaying to the rhythm of the gospel tune, Spicey sang "Harps from the Tomb" with the others. She could hear Ezra's voice, and although he be singin' like he on stage, his tone a little off.

Suddenly Miss Carrie came a running out of the house, across the portico and down the steps. She hustled faster than Spicey thunk possible, being a genteel lady and all.

Spicey turned to run affer her, but Betsey caught her 'round the waist just as Ezra stepped forward with his arms out and eyes showing concern. Betsey turned Spicey away and said, "Let her be."

Spicey wasn't sure Betsey spoke to Ezra or to her.

ୠୠୠ

The *slam* of the swinging door smacking against the frame was not loud enough to block Mama's wails or the dirge the slaves sung in the yard. Caroline darted across the portico, down the steps, and kept going. Not knowing where she was headed or when she'd stop.

A heaviness grew in her chest as she ran down Gibson Branch Road past peanut fields and the old cemetery where Sarah would soon be buried. Her sides burned with cramping pains, her corset cut into her skin, and her black, heavy autumn skirts flapped loudly in the cool air, threatening to trip her. She pulled them from between her legs and held them high as she continued on.

She didn't know how far she'd gone, but she felt like the bones in her feet and legs had liquefied. She stumbled, falling hard on knees covered only by thin cotton drawers. Her skirts splayed out around her, and she collapsed on the dirt path. Small stones scratched her face. Pain shot from bleeding wounds on her knees that soaked her drawers and petticoats. Too weak to pull herself up, she lay in the dirt, breathing hard.

The great heaviness in her chest grew fuller, burying itself deeper into her body, and finally came out in great, quaking sobs. She retched over and over, then laid her head down—too weak to move. The foul smell of vomit made her stomach convulse again, but there was nothing to bring up. It took all her strength to roll away from the putrid smell.

"Why?" She brought her knees to her chest and cried out, "If you're a loving God, why take my sister?"

CHAPTER SEVEN

November 15, 1859

Caroline dreamed of Sarah dressed in a white linen gown. Her small body lay stiff on the foyer table, her face pure and soft as cotton. In a circle around her, slaves swayed and wailed their mournful hymns.

Sarah's presence still felt real as Caroline awakened. She reached out to touch Sarah but found only air. Her hand grasped nothing. Gone. Sarah gone forever. She rolled to her side and her face sunk into the cold pillow wet with tears shed during the dream. The bedchamber remained in silent, chilly shadows.

She closed her eyes and concentrated on listening for the sounds of the house but heard nothing. No one was up and moving. Relieved to hide for a few more minutes under the warmth of her two quilts—one hers, the other Sarah's—she gathered them tightly around her. The quilts hugged her body, embracing her in a field of sewn flowers and vines, bringing her closer to her sister. She nestled deeper into the feather tick, grateful for this time of morning when she could have her privacy. Solitude was rare in the Gibson household, and her bed became her personal refuge, despite Spicey asleep close by on a floor pallet.

With the dark, early morning about her and dreams of Sarah still squeezing her heart, Caroline was reminded of what Mama had said the previous evening; that the closest thing she could compare to death was the time of daybreak when there seemed to be no sound. The birds in their nests had not yet been awakened by the first glint of light. There was an expectation of a new beginning, only moments away. Just as morning turns into day, day turns into night, everything following in a circle, renewed once again. She hoped Mama was right and somehow the new beginning, whenever it came, would be healing.

Mama had never taken her children to worship between church walls, but she occasionally read to them from the Bible. She had her own personal religion. Her beliefs reached back to ancestors on the Simmons family tree. There were even rumors of Hebrew blood in her veins, but such things weren't talked about in the Christian South of Onslow County. Only Caroline's preacher friend, John, seemed to be intrigued by the idea. Still, Caroline knew there was something different about Mama. Even though she rarely attended church, her deep faith guided everything she did and said. Seemed not a day went by without her teaching Caroline of this or that herb, animal, or person being put here on earth, "By the good hands of God, praise be to the Almighty."

Mama had taught her falsehoods. The good hands of God had not saved Sarah.

Having drifted off to sleep again, Caroline awoke later to the comforting smells of coffee brewing and biscuits baking. She peeked over the side of her bed and wasn't surprised to see Spicey's empty pallet. The girl must have gone to relieve herself.

Caroline threw off her quilts. Her feet hit the cold floor, she shivered, then scampered to her dressing table where she perched on a cushioned bench and put her feet on a rung off the chilled planks. Removing the glass chimney of a kerosene lamp, she lit the wick, blew out the lucifer, and lowered the height of the flame.

The black crepe had been taken off the mirror on her dressing table, but her perfume bottles were still tied with black ribbons. Looking in the mirror, Caroline pulled her bed cap from her braids and let them fall over her shoulders. She glanced at the clock and waited impatiently for Spicey's morning ministrations. Shaking from the cold, she wrapped her arms around herself. It always seemed colder in the country than in town. Perhaps because the plantation house was much larger than their town home. Surely it wasn't warmer on the coast, but there was something about the way the homes were nestled near each other in Swansboro. They'd never stayed at White Oak Plantation this late into autumn. Papa said they wouldn't go into town until Mama was done grieving.

Where was Spicey?

Never having gotten herself ready for the day, Caroline passed the time by opening drawers. In one, she found a black silk snood she thought appropriate to wear over her hair.

A beam of light grew through the opening of the bedchamber door as Spicey pushed her petite body through. She was already in a gray dress and a crisp white apron. Her long, curly hair, tied back with an orange ribbon, never stayed where it belonged. The slave girl held a small pine knot burning on a tin in one hand while she hugged a pitcher of water to pour into a washbasin. "Miss Carrie, Mistress is askin' for ya."

"Then quickly come wash me and get my hair done." Caroline squared her shoulders and handed the snood to Spicey.

A half-hour later, Caroline stepped into the dining room where Mama stood tall and slim, mahogany-colored hair pulled up with a few ringlets framing the coiffure. Dressed in a black satin mourning gown, she stared out the window where the sunrise fought its rays through morning mists.

With nine house slaves and over twenty field slaves, Mama spent much of her time managing her household and the demands of those in the quarter. She saw to the needs of food, clothing, doctoring, and orchestrating her slaves' responsibilities. She even delivered their babies, which was not the custom. Mama had been raised on a plantation, like generations of women before her. For her five daughters, she held to southern practices of letting them be idle. She gave them only small tasks, while also teaching them to embroider, tat, and play the piano. She wanted them raised as genteel.

Caroline didn't mind small tasks. They helped her pass the long days in the country. The slaves did the hard labor, which suited her fine. She kissed Mama's cheek, as expected. "Good morning, Mama." Her voice, void of feeling, came with a pang of guilt. Mama needed as much comfort as she.

"Good morning, Carrie." Mama turned away from the window. Her black hooped skirts twirled a little farther than she, then came back to settle in front of her. She didn't seem to notice her daughter's dark mood and broke from her own melancholia. "Betsey's down with arthritic swellings this morning, and she sent Cozy to cook our meal. I was hoping for Betsey's help, but I will get none." Mama shook her head and sighed. "After breakfast, will you go out to the greater garden and see what pumpkins we have? I'd like to make Julia a comfort basket, seeing as her time to deliver is so near. Your father will be going into Swansboro today and said he'd check on her."

Caroline's heart quickened at the thought of perhaps also seeing John. It'd been far too long since she'd seen him. The more time she spent with the reverend, the more she'd felt incomplete without him. "May I go with Papa? Why must we stay so long in the country?"

Mama looked to the floor, but not quickly enough to hide the sorrow in her dark eyes.

A bite of regret tightened Caroline's jaw. It was wrong to push Mama when she grieved. "Forgive me, Mama. I'll not ask again."

Steps echoed from the hall. Papa soon stood before them. "Shall we sit for breakfast?"

Mama and Caroline sat. In the hall, Hester could be heard reprimanding Benny for leaving his marbles on the floor. They entered the room, gave Mama a kiss on the cheek, and took their customary places. Sarah's abandoned chair created an ache in Caroline's heart. She quickly looked away.

"Betsey!" Papa called out.

"Betsey's not well, but young Cozy will serve," Mama explained.

Cozy came into the dining room, her large lips pressed together, an indigo scarf wrapped and tied on her head. She carried an extravagant silver tray with breakfast upon it. She slowly walked to the sideboard, carefully unburdening herself of the large tray, then spooned sausage and gravy over a biscuit on a plate, adding other delicacies.

Papa said nothing more.

His unusual silence disturbed Caroline. He had said little the last few weeks since Sarah's death.

"Sure was cold last night." Hester seemed to want conversation. "Can I turn your thoughts toward moving into town?"

Papa grunted then glanced toward Mama who appeared to have not heard a thing.

Caroline could only agree with Hester. She'd never see John this far out in the country.

Cozy set Papa's plate before him. Steam rose off the gravy.

Benny watched Cozy serve, wiggling in his chair and anxious to eat his meal. But as youngest, he'd be served last.

"Autumn is truly upon us." Hester tried again for repartee, but the words were meaningless, as the conversation had been the last few weeks in the void of Sarah's absence. Hester shrugged.

Sadness filled the space between them.

ଓଽଓଽଓଽ

A short time later, Caroline stepped onto the back porch. The cool air smelled of chimney smoke from slave row, but the crispness felt refreshing after the quiet stuffiness of the family breakfast. In the early morning light, she found a basket hanging on a fence post of the kitchen garden.

Walking toward the greater garden, her feet crunched onto frozen earth which had been mud the day before. Out in the fields, autumn rains had coerced their way into making brown, muddy gulches, now frosty and solid. Fog still clung to the trees; the world painted shades of gray.

In the distance, a small part of Papa's eight-hundred acres, were fields of broken-down plant stalks. Small flecks of sodden cotton—too tiny to be picked—clung to naked branches. The dead stalks and brown earth were ready to be overturned. All spoke of death.

She crunched her way to the garden. When she passed the open doors of the barn, the sour stench of cow dung burned her nostrils. Moses, Joe, and Big George stood by the big double-doors. "Morning." She gave them a tip of her head.

"Mornin' Miz Caroline," they replied in unison.

Restless with heavy udders, a cow inside shuffled, mooing at a high pitch, as cows often did before being milked. Steaming clouds of breath flowed from all the cows' nostrils. One of the slaves, Joe, who had tribal markings slashed on his cheeks and forehead, walked away with a wooden pail in hand, prepared to milk the last cow. The other men stepped toward the house with full pails, whisps of vapor coming off the yellowy-white liquid.

Ten yards farther, Caroline passed the empty tobacco drying barn and then the cooper's shed where barrels were built to hold the turpentine distilled from the long leaf pine trees surrounding their fields. A steam saw, dairy house, smokehouse and building that housed a cotton gin lay behind the cooper's shed, softly covered in misty fog. The greater garden lay well past the outbuildings, to best gather the most sun on fine days, yet close enough to Gibson Branch Creek to enable the slaves to water it easily. Over forty people depended on its abundance.

On this gloomy morning, the sun in the east had not yet spread its rays across the frosty plants.

Caroline shivered and pulled her shawl closer, knotting it. As she moved through the rows of pumpkins and blackened squash vines, her skirts caught on the tendrils. Fortuitously, she'd left her hoops hanging from a hook in her bedchamber. Still, she wished Betsey was well enough to do the cutting herself. Wasn't it time to bring all the pumpkins into the cellar? She sighed and cut the prickly stem of the closest pumpkin.

Why couldn't Mama understand going into town would help Caroline's mood? Talking to John would help even more. She needed his friendship. He always seemed to know how to comfort her. John, a never-changing rock where Caroline found a place to rest no matter the storm, was far from where she needed him to be. He'd taught her of Christianity and helped her realize it was what was missing in her life. The shared experience of student and teacher of gospel had brought them closer. So, would he understand that she now couldn't help but question the existence of God? Shame hitched her breath.

Once the cooking was completed, Mama handed Caroline the comfort basket with a pumpkin pie and other foods and concoctions. "Ride into town with Papa and take this to Julia."

The first smile spread across Caroline's face since Sarah's death. "Oh, thank you, Mama."

Mama abruptly walked away, probably feeling a bit anxious about not being in town with her pregnant daughter Julia. Did Mama blame herself for Sarah's death? Caroline suspected in some way, *she* blamed Mama and God both.

Glad to leave Mama's gray and forlorn presence, Caroline looked forward to spending hours in the carriage with Papa as they traveled. More important, she hoped to find an excuse to visit John.

Moving into town was what they all needed. Caroline mentioned this to Papa as they traveled in the buggy.

He smiled sadly. "You may be right, little lamb."

Caroline loved her father and missed their conversations. Normally an attentive, affectionate man, he often made it known his children were his treasures. He worked hard to support his family. Through some bad experiences, he learned early in his planting career that he didn't care to employ an overseer but rather act as overseer himself and use trustworthy slaves to be what he called his "drivers" to keep the field hands on task. Because of Papa's function as overseer, the family rarely saw him during the day. But in the evenings, they gathered in the parlor for games or listened to Caroline play the piano.

Caroline leaned against Papa's shoulder. He smelled of freshly pressed linen. An aroma as familiar as Betsey's biscuits. "How much longer must we stay at White Oak?"

"Your mother will decide. She's delivered all her grandbabies so far. I suspect we'll make the move when Julia asks her to come."

Papa shifted the reins to his left hand and wrapped his right arm around Caroline's shoulders. "Don't pester your mama about the move. She needs time to grieve."

Being in Papa's embrace gave her the comfort she'd been missing. "Can't she grieve in town?"

"Death is a social event. She's not ready to face her friends and neighbors or the feelings they may expose." Papa stroked her arm. "Be patient. She's the strongest woman I know and will recover with time."

Papa's patience left Caroline frustrated. "Should not her God give her the comfort she needs?"

"*Her* God?" Papa's eyes narrowed; Caroline's hostility obviously not lost on him. "Have you decided He's not *your* God too?"

"I can't rightly say anymore." She hesitated, suddenly feeling timid. "If there is a God, He's forgotten us," she said a little above a whisper.

"We've spoken before of my beliefs—or should I say lack of beliefs. I've never been sure there's a God." Papa spoke cautiously. "For some reason, it saddens me to hear you questioning His existence."

Caroline couldn't bring herself to talk any further on the subject. If she did, she'd have to explain how Sarah's suffering brought bitterness into her heart and anger toward Mama. Caroline preferred to not examine those feelings too closely.

They made a stop on the banks of Starkey's Creek at Sander's Landing, where Papa's Negroes had brought wagons with his barrels of turpentine, pitch, barrel staves, planks, and other lumber.

Papa walked over to inspect the piles of pine products that were to be put on barges to float down the White Oak River to Swansboro where they'd be either stored in his warehouse or sent to his ships. The ships would take the goods to the West Indies and trade them for sugar, molasses, honey, and fruits. The ships would then catch the Gulf Stream currents to the North American cities of Boston, New York, and Philadelphia where the commodities could be sold.

Caroline and Papa stopped again only briefly to eat the dinner Cozy had packed and to water the horse. They were making good time. Although sore from the wooden seat, Caroline didn't complain about the fast pace. She hoped they'd arrive in Swansboro before early afternoon, so she'd have time to visit with John after delivering Mama's basket to Julia.

They'd stopped on the old Mattocks land at the White Oak River's edge. Caroline knew the area well. It was a common place for travelers to water horses because there was no riverbank, just a slope of soft dirt like a beach. She stood in Onslow County, but the land on the other side of the river was Carteret County.

She climbed a nearby rise and found the modest cemetery to be where she'd remembered. There was only a half-dozen headstones. The biggest one belonged to John's grandfather. She stood in front of it. *In memory of John Mattocks who departed this life 18th day of May 1828. Aged 63 years.* The bones of a man she'd never known lay beneath her feet. But his name was the same as the man she hoped to know better.

"Caroline, we need to be on our way," Papa called.

She joined him at the river's edge, where the current flowed slow and served as a swimming hole on hot summer days. This same river ran near both White Oak Plantation and their town house in Swansboro. When she was younger, she'd loved to float in the river and let it take her where it would with no determined path. She missed those days when her sisters, Julia and Mary were still living at home. It'd been seven years since Julia left and over two years for Mary. Both had children of their own. Now the oldest child living at White Oak, when would Caroline's turn come to marry and start a family? She hoped soon.

CHAPTER EIGHT

Swansboro, Onslow County

Caroline's town house, as most southern homes, had a name. Known as Gibson House, it stood atop the brow of a hill overlooking the wide expanse of the White Oak River where the river entered the sound, then flowed to the ocean.

As the carriage neared, the land behind the house came into view. It swept down a soft green slope to the water's shore. Papa's schooner floated at the dock, waves lapping at its side. Also nestled on the property were small stables, a poultry yard, an old windmill, beehives, and a few Negro cabins on its farthest border to the north.

The sky clear where Bogue Sound met the mouth of the White Oak River, a few fishing boats headed toward shore. November meant fishing season would soon be over. The Atlantic Ocean lay two miles distant, and no fishermen would be out that far this late in the day.

"Good evening, Caleb," Papa called to the neighbor across the street.

"Y'all in for the winter?"

"No, just here one evening."

One evening was enough to lift Caroline's mood. She loved Swansboro. The town bustled with people, and although she was shy, her sisters often took her to soirees and teas at their friends' homes.

"Sorry to hear of your little one," Caleb called as they came to a stop in front of their home.

Papa tilted his hat in acknowledgment.

Caroline stepped from the carriage, then greeted by Zylphia, one of the slaves who cared for the town house in their absence.

"Welcome back, Miz Caroline." Zylphia curtsied.

"Thank you, kindly. My satchel will be brought in shortly." Caroline entered her home, one of the biggest in Swansboro, but not as ostentatious in name or manner as the White Oak Plantation home. Gibson House was a lovely white home with piazzas running its length both front and back. It had eight rooms and a cookhouse with a covered catwalk.

After settling affairs with Zylphia, Caroline walked across the street to Julia's house, a town house kitty-corner to Gibson House. Both Georgian, the homes were built near the same year and in the same manner when Swansboro was in its infancy almost a hundred years before.

Caroline knocked.

Julia's slave Esther answered the door. "Affernoon, Miz Caroline. Nice to see ya in town."

"Obliged, Esther."

She backed away and gestured Caroline to enter. Looking to the floor she kept a thin smile on her face, deliberately not showing her teeth. They were rotten.

Inside, Caroline found Billy and Edgar playing cup-and-ball on the floor in the center passage. "Where's your Mama, boys?" She knelt and set the basket on the floor while giving each of her nephews a kiss on the top of their heads.

"Lyin' down," Billy whispered, pointing up the stairs. "Told us to play quiet or she'd take a switch to us."

Caroline found her sister upstairs, reclined on her massive gold and red velvet-covered bed. The bed panels were of the same velvet, draped from mahogany posts and rails. Heavy damask portieres had been pulled over both windows, giving the bedchamber a golden glow. The room smelled of lavender and the soapy musk of furniture cleaner.

"Oh, Carrie! I missed you so." Julia pushed herself to sitting, as if she pulled a barrel upright. "Did all y'all come into town?" Her face flushed with exertion, her breathing sounded labored, even though it appeared she'd been resting. Her thick, brown hair had been expertly coiffured and pulled into a black lace snood. Although nine months enceinte, her skin, soft as cream, still showed her lovely, curved features. There was no one in town more beautiful than Julia. People often talked of the five attractive Gibson sisters, but it was always Julia they raved over.

The back of Caroline's eyes burned. It was now *four* Gibson sisters. She swallowed hard and tried to move her mind elsewhere. "No, just Papa and me. We'll return to White Oak tomorrow." She hugged her sister. "Mama's still grieving. She's worried about you though and had me carry over this here comfort basket." Caroline put the basket on Julia's lap—or rather, what was left of her lap.

"Tell me Betsey's buttermilk cake is in here."

Caroline grinned. "Betsey was down today. Cozy made you a pumpkin pie."

"Almost as good. Wish I could find a slave who knew how to cook like Betsey. It's so hard to find decent servants. The whole lot of 'em are lazy."

Julia wouldn't expect Caroline to comment. She often talked without anyone's input. Maybe that was why Caroline had let her sister carry the conversations for years.

Julia continued going through the basket's contents. "Looks like some of Mama's remedies are in here. Sweet thing!" A sad smile flickered. "I don't believe anything can cure what ails me but delivering this babe." Sighing, she dropped the basket to the floor, leaning back into the cushions of her luxurious bed. "Sugar, would you mind much asking Esther to bring me some sweet tea?"

ೞೞೞ

The church stood down the street from Julia's. Caroline hoped she'd find John there because she wasn't sure where he was living. His small salary kept him moving often, sometimes living in homes of his parishioners. About a year ago, he'd given up his family's wealth to become a preacher.

The cold air hit her face and hands first, and she shivered. She'd forgotten her gloves. The smell of the ocean was in the wind, and her black skirts blew behind her like a sail on one of Papa's schooners.

The wind swirled around her and seemed to whisper misgivings like a naughty antagonist, giving her reservations about discussing her doubts regarding God with John. She should probably turn around and go back to Julia's, but her desire to be close to John was stronger than her desire to avoid the conversation and pulled her forward.

As she walked, she considered not telling him the whole truth so he wouldn't see her failings. Only recently had they become good friends, and she didn't want to jeopardize that. John was three years older and had spent many of the last five years away from home. They'd been mere acquaintances before his travels. She blessed the day his brother Ned married her sister Mary two years before.

After Ned and Mary's union, visits between the Mattocks and Gibsons became more frequent. John and Caroline found themselves together, usually in deep conversation about his travels and her interests in faraway cultures. And then he started teaching her his Christian beliefs. He had a passion she'd rarely witnessed in men and expressed his views freely, seemingly without a care of disapproval.

Caroline had soon realized she wanted to be with him more often. She wasn't sure he felt the same and, subsequently, she'd become awkward around him. In the past, when they'd talked, she'd looked him in the eyes. Now she found she didn't know where to look—afraid of what he might discover in her eyes. The last she'd spent time with him, she couldn't concentrate on what he'd told her, her mind had wandered so—her imagination had them courting and falling in love. If only she could express her feelings better.

When in town the winter before, Caroline, with Mary and Ned, had often attended John's church services. His sermons were as passionately delivered as his private conversations and had her wondering if religion was a missing piece in her life.

Her relationship with God had always been very general and uncertain. Mama taught her how to pray as a child, but never expected her to do it. When she prayed now, it was often at Spicey's request. Caroline wondered if she was silly or just hopeful that some unseen force could affect her life. Her prayers for Sarah certainly hadn't been answered.

As Caroline walked and thought about John, she realized she could never get enough of his gentle temperament, even if she didn't have a strong belief in all he taught. He somehow gave her the desire to become someone better.

The church stood before her. Taking a deep breath and placing a hand over her racing heart, she walked up the steps, opened the door, and entered the small assembly hall.

There was no one inside. The room was solemnly quiet, as if reverence existed even without anyone to witness.

She sighed heavily. She wouldn't be seeing John after all. She decided to stay, get warm, and try to find peace in her heart. Closing the door, she removed her bonnet and hung it on a peg. Even though her hopes for seeing John were thwarted, her hands still shook. She rubbed them together, trying to warm up.

The low sun threw jewel-toned colors from the stained-glass windows across the vacant pews. She imagined John behind the pulpit. He seemed to give it life. Caroline suddenly felt uncomfortable and hollow in this holy place as she realized God knew her doubts. She was a sinner in His house. She stepped back and turned to leave.

"Good afternoon, Caroline. I'm glad you came in today."

She jumped at John's voice. In a back alcove by a window, he sat at a table with Bible and papers spread before him.

"You startled me. I thought the church empty." She didn't move toward him. Her chest constricted, and her face flushed with warmth.

"I was studying for the youth lesson tomorrow. Can I help you with anything?" His wavy brown hair was smoothed back, as if he'd been raking his hands through it, his face clean shaven, his jaw square and strong.

Caroline decided she couldn't tell him her doubts about God after all. "I was over at Julia's and thought I'd take a walk. It's windy outside, and the church looked like good shelter." After the words left her lips, she heard the lie she'd just told in God's house. A horrible reprobate, she gazed at the wood floor, dark and worn with age.

"The Church will shelter you from many storms." John got up and moved toward her.

Did he know why she came? Suddenly nervous, she took shorter breaths. "It's cold out." Embarrassed by her repetition and small talk, she didn't know what next to say and kept glancing at the floor.

"My deepest sympathies regarding Sarah." John's eyes showed genuine concern. Only a few yards from her, he continued to move forward. "I received your letter and prayed for her and you." He cleared his throat. "I was out of town when she passed, or I would've come. How are your parents?"

Now close enough to touch her, he did not.

She wished he would. Could he hear her thudding heart?

"They're having a hard time, John . . . I mean, Reverend Mattocks." She hadn't called him John since they were young children, and her face burned with the embarrassment of presuming the old familiarity.

"John. Please. We've been friends a long time. And we're family now since Ned and Mary wed."

Glad for his recognition of their friendship, she gave him a small smile, but not being able to control her emotions with him so near, she lost some of her resolve and took a small step back. "Maybe I do need to talk to you." She couldn't look away from his dark, almost black eyes. She cleared her throat. "But I'm not sure if I'm coming to you as a friend or a clergyman."

"To me there's no difference." His smile like sunshine in a shady place confirmed his words, compassion visible in his wide-set eyes.

A fleeting hope went through her mind that maybe he could be as captivated by her as she to him. Did he not feel the currents of attraction between them? Flutters rose in her stomach. Here she was about to tell him her deepest feelings about God, and she knew he'd disapprove. He'd think her childish and sinful. Then what if he didn't like her?

She glanced away in case her eyes betrayed her thoughts. "My parents are usually in Swansboro by the end of October, but they'll not come into town. I fret about them keeping to themselves at White Oak. Mama doesn't want to receive sympathy from the townsfolk. I fear my parents are depressed in spirit." Caroline glanced at John's eyes, trying to discern his feelings. She shouldn't be talking about her parents. They wouldn't approve, and it wasn't why she'd searched him out.

"I'd be happy to meet with your parents, but let's talk about you." He stood within inches; his words spoken softly.

Caroline had to strain to hear. Her heart skipped. For an instant, she held her breath.

He took her cold hand, the warmth bringing comfort.

His generous words, directed solely at her, broke the dam of resolve and made her sorrow come to the forefront—her misgivings forgotten. Her shoulders dropped. Tired of being alone in her grief, she needed him.

John's compassionate brown eyes kept her gaze steady.

"You should've seen Sarah, John. I can't get the image out of my mind. No little girl should go through such suffering." With the memory of Sarah's fevered, tortured body lying on her bed came a lump in Caroline's throat. She didn't want to cry and willed her tears away.

"It breaks my heart to hear you speak of it and see the pain in your eyes. If I could take this from you, I would." His sympathy was genuine and his concern for her made her feel a little lightheaded.

"I thought I believed in God." She swallowed, her throat closing. "Sarah's suffering and death has made me think He cannot exist." There. She'd said it aloud, even if she'd winced with each word. Disgusted by her lack of faith, would John now release her hand and walk away? He probably thought less of her. She certainly thought less of herself.

But his eyes showed no alarm. He didn't walk away. He continued to hold her gaze and her hand. "Sometimes you have to lean on someone else's faith to get yourself through sorrow. It's not a time to decide God's existence. But the last thing I want to do is preach a sermon to you." He squeezed her hand and gave a half-smile that showed a dimple. "Please feel free to lean on me now. I've learned peace comes from loving God. Peace is one of the greatest blessings Man can receive, but it's not a gift. It needs to be earned by having faith and following in God's ways."

She did want to lean on John. She daringly but gently gripped his hand. Her body felt weary, and she wanted him to hold her. "But how do you keep your faith? How could there be a God?

Why did He let me and Sarah feel such pain? I thought He was supposed to love us." With each question, Caroline's voice rose.

John's sad eyes pierced her soul. He drew closer.

She could smell his wool suit and the soap he'd used to lather and shave that morning. She could no longer keep her eyes from spilling over with tears. It happened in an instant—she leaned toward him as if pulled by a magnet and was suddenly in his arms and felt the warmth of his body.

One of his hands pressed firmly into the small of her back, the other gently moved the hair off her shoulder.

It wasn't just she who moved forward, but him too. He held her by his *own* will. And dare she believe desires?

"Never can peace and confusion abide in the same soul." His breath brushed her skin as he spoke soothingly. "I know death seems like the worst thing right now, but spiritual death will leave you hollow forever. Somehow over time, we recover from losing our loved ones. I never looked at it this way before, but I now see losing my brother when I was not yet six as a blessing. Perhaps, I should be relieved my father died when I was three? I can hardly remember the sorrow of losing them. It does still cling to my mother, however. And I can see what Sarah's death is doing to you. Let me help you, Caroline."

Although she willed it not to happen, she couldn't stop the sobs. How could she allow John to see her this way? Yet, she didn't want to pull away. At that moment, she never wanted to be parted from him again. Never had she experienced such comfort. This man of God was tender, and her heart expanded with his affection.

CHAPTER NINE

November 20, 1859

Well into November, a month past Miss Sarah dying, Spicey couldn't reckon who hurting more—Miss Carrie for grieving over her sister in that cold earth out by the county road or her Mama, Mistress Gibson, for not being able to save the girl.

Lying on her shivery floor pallet, Spicey didn't want to be leaving her blankets to get up and stir the embers in the hearth and add another log. Autumn done brung the night dark on early, and Spicey not tired enough to sleep. She wanted to stay in bed for the warmth all the same.

Miss Carrie was in bed next to Spicey. Sarah's quilt peeked out from under Miss Carrie's quilt. Spicey made it up with the bed each morning. Looking at the dim underside of Miss Carrie's bed, ropes crisscrossed, tied to the bed rails, holding up Miss Carrie and her ticking. What must it feel like to sleep on a tick of softest goose feathers?

Spicey pushed that thinking out of her head and ruminated on the *bump, bump, bump* in her chest. It was the way she checked her heart to see if it kept time with her thoughts. She didn't rightly understand how it kept time and not stop its beating. It was like it had its own massa. Right now, she felt it needed some tender words to sooth its sadness. She missed talkative Miss Sarah too. No one seemed to notice how the house slaves was grievin'.

When Miss Carrie went to church last winter when in town, Spicey waited outside on the porch as usual, but she could hear that young preacher's loud and caring voice. Loud and caring don't rightly go together, but his voice were like when your mam thinks you lost, and she callin' your name with love and worryment.

He up at that pulpit speaking all kind of curious words. He spoke about a mighty change of heart, and Spicey done thunk on that ever since. He beseeched the white folk to bind their hearts to the Savior, and then the Lord Jesus would write on their hearts. Spicey tossed those words 'round an 'round in her head and ain't quite got the understandin' of them yet.

She listened to Miss Carrie's breathing to determine if she be awake. She were, so Spicey asked, "Whatcha think the preacher meant by binding and writing on our hearts, cuz my heart jus' stays in my chest, tickin' like the grandfather clock in the main hall?"

Miss Carrie warmed to the question right away, rolling toward Spicey and reaching for her hand. But that her way at night when the room too dark and to see Spicey's black face. It's like time hopped back and they were young'uns again, before Mistress and Massa Gibson kept reminding Miss Carrie that she need to remember the rules and keep Spicey in her place. Spicey suppose she should keep her heart big and open and not be angry at them for that.

"Well, I think Reverend Mattocks was referring to not sinning anymore." She gave a little laugh like a hiccup, which surprised Spicey cuz of how sad Miss Carrie be of late. "He sure does look fine up there at the pulpit." She sounded all funny in her voice.

"You sweet on that preacher?" Spicey asked, disappointed some that Miss Carrie changed the subject. Spicey really wanted to know 'bout what the Reverend said 'bout writing on hearts.

Miss Carrie looked over the edge of the bed and in the soft glow from the embers, Spicey could see Miss Carrie smile, and it felt like she be the sister Spicey always hoped to have. "Don't tell no one, you hear, but he took me in his arms last week, and I about swooned. Oh Spicey," she said all out of breath, "I think I'm in love."

They both giggled then, but affer the giggling was over, fear crawled into that beating heart of Spicey's. If Miss Carrie marry, where will Spicey live? If Miss Carrie love, will Spicey be torn from love?

ଔଔଔ

In the backyard, with field slaves lined up for their weekly allowances, Spicey watched Hanna glare at sweet Betsey.

"Ya uppity ole nigra think yo better dan me?" Hanna jutted out her sharp chin, her cheekbones and nose just as pointy.

Betsey gave no comeback as she placed a cloth sack of cornmeal, pound of pork belly, bread loaf, small crock buttermilk, and about a fist size of sugar in Hanna's basket.

Miss Carrie say we's got sugar in abundance cuz Massa Gibson in shipping trade with the plantations in the West Indies. Other plantation slaves here-bouts don't get no sugar, onliest molasses.

Hanna was just spouting. The field slave got spite cuz house slaves eat good tastin' leftovers in the big house and ain't given weekly allowances of victuals.

Short Betsey looked up to stare Hanna in the eye like she had no time to mess with her sass. "I'm doin' my job jus' as you's doing your'n."

Hanna appeared as if fire gonna come outta her mouth, but she clamped it shut and shot a look over Betsey's head.

Spicey turned and caught-on Mistress Gibson had stepped onto the porch.

Mistress, dressed all in black, stand tall and erect as a fine lady, but sadness draped her like she about to fall down and die herself. Putting a daughter in the ground seem more than she can bear. She a good mistress, and Spicey had been hoping Mistress Gibson would come back to who she be before Miss Sarah got sick.

Hanna stepped to Spicey with her eyes on her shoes, and Spicey placed a winter dress of double-weave homespun cotton on top of the food in her basket.

Spicey's first duties were always to Miss Carrie—cleaning her room, sewing her underclothes, linens, and bedclothes, and caring for her clothing, body and hair, and anything else that she asked.

For the plantation, Spicey spun cotton and made goods, such as clothing for the field slaves. It hard work, but she liked spinning the cotton, weaving at the loom, and using her hands to make things.

Hanna walked off, and the next fieldslave in line stepped up to Spicey and asked, "Dat wo'n till dreads."

Spicey ain't get the girl's meaning. Some field slave talk Spicey couldn't reckon, even though she raised with Ole Pearl on slave row till Spicey be four. Ole Pearl too ancient to have vision no more, but long time back, she minded all the mams' chilluns while they worked the fields or in the big house. Spicey's mam was the Mammy, but she gone now, buried out back of the quarter.

"Whatcha ax?" Spicey said to the fieldslave in front of her, who shook her head and walked off. Spicey shrugged and glanced back at Mistress Gibson.

She there watching the goings-on, saying nothin'.

Betsey settled another bag of cornmeal and food stuffs in a basket, her movements slow and careful. The red swellings on her fingers looked angry, like they hurt something awful, but Spicey never heared Betsey complaining none.

The cook and boss over house slaves, Betsey do other chores like doling out Sunday allowances too. She the closest thing Spicey had to a mam since hers died two years past. She couldn't reckon why Hanna be ornery to Betsey, cuz she about the sweetest thing on the plantation. Never say a bad word to no one.

If Spicey tell Betsey "I's just too tired to launder another petticoat," Betsey say with a grin, "Be glad ya ain't launderin' gowns." If Spicey tells Betsey, "My back hurts from sleepin' on a floor pallet," Betsey say, "Be content ya ain't livin' on slave row." Betsey always lookin' for the positive. She sure easy to love.

Ezra stepped up for his rations from Betsey, making something in Spicey's chest flutter like a butterfly.

Betsey placed his allowance in a basket hanging from his muscled arm, her bronzed skin light against Ezra's inky brown.

When he stepped to Spicey next, he cleared his throat.

She felt her face grow hot when she set woolen stockings and long johns of unbleached coarse linen in his outstretched hands. Why she reacts such? He ain't one to admire.

"I thank ya, Spicey," is all he said afore stepping away, but it was the first time he'd said her name. He said it all warm like.

But then a wind blew and chilled Spicey.

The slaves in line wrapped their arms around theyselves. Stink of decayin' leaves came with the breeze. Other than the pines, most the trees reached out, skeletal like.

Good time to dole out winter clothes. Spicey's own, and all the female house slaves, had hand-me-down clothes from the Massa's womenfolk, fixed to fit without corset or hoops. Spicey made all the aprons they got on. They considered a pros'prous plantation with over thirty slaves and hundreds of acres for crops.

Spicey wasn't bought. She born here, as was her mam. Gibsons have slaves for many generations. Ole Pearl come with Mistress Gibson from her Simmons plantation, where they had slaves for generations, likewise.

Cozy was in charge of the poultry and dairy houses and tending the kitchen garden. She helps Betsey with the cooking. She eighteen like Spicey, but they don't see each other much, just mealtime.

"We're going fishing, Mama," Little Massa Benny called as he ran by with his slave, Jess, both toting fishing poles.

Spicey 'spose they headin' to Gibson Branch Crick. Little Massa Benny the onliest son of Mistress and Massa. The house used to be full of daughters, but two married, and now Sarah gone. Miss Carrie eighteen and the oldest now, then Hester, two years younger. Family getting smaller all the time.

Out passed where the boys run off, Spicey spied a carriage coming their way. Mistress Gibson move down the steps with a lil' interest in her eyes. It's good to know she not dead inside.

The carriage pulled up, and Massa Harget descended and gave polite "how do" to all as his slave tugged the horse and carriage off to the stables.

He walked with a gold stick, but Spicey couldn't see why. Although plump, he 'peared to have two strong legs.

"I've come to bring the joyous news of your daughter delivering a healthy girl."

Mistress Gibson's smile sweeter than flowers, and Spicey felt like the world come back to itself.

"How is she feeling, Daniel?" Mistress asked.

"You know Julia. She's ready to plan a party and wear her newest gown." His mustache spread when he grinned wide, him pleased with his wife and child both.

"Come in and tell me more." Mistress took his arm.

They walked into the house, and Spicey heared her sayin' they'd all be goin' to Swansboro first thing next week.

That mean Miss Carrie see her man—the Reverend. How long afore Spicey lose Miss Carrie?

CHAPTER TEN

November 21-23, 1859

Today the sky more white than blue. Pale sunshine seeped through the open double doors of the old cookhouse but ain't warmin' Spicey none. She glad to have her hands in hot, soapy water.

Washing day usually Wednesday, but today be Monday, and they all be getting ready to head to Swansboro in two days' time. From the big house, she heared the paddles clear down yonder at the crick where the slaves beat wet clothes and linens dirtless against a block. A fine place to do the every-day washing but mighty cold in that crick in November. Druthers than take a beating to the expensive gowns, Spicey scrubbed them in the cookhouse in big tubs filled with warm water, washing real gentle like. Miss Carrie love her fancy dresses, just like all the womenfolk at White Oak.

Betsey brought more warm water and poured it from the big copper kettle into Spicey's tub. "Ya best scrub a might faster seein' as ya have five mo' gowns here."

"I knowed that. 'Haps iffen Cozy come she can help me some?" Spicey asked with a hopeful lilt to her voice.

"Cozy got her own extra chores of crating the chickens." Betsey walked back to the stove, scooped more water from the rain barrel into the kettle, replaced the lid, and moved to her worktable to knead bread.

Behind her, Mistress Gibson's jars of herbs and remedies were up against the wall on shelves. She always trying to keep everyone healthy on the plantation, white and black. Like a mam should.

Careful while scrubbing the lace cuffs, Spicey thunk more on who her family be. She reckoned Miss Carrie bound to marry soon, even iffen tain't the preacher. But would Spicey move to Miss Carrie's new home? She won't want Spicey sleeping near the marriage bed. Might be Miss Carrie leave Spicey at the plantation, and she have to move to the quarter?

Could she lower herself to marry Ezra, a despised slave driver? He not a houseslave like she raised to be. She'd be marrying down, but she mayhap wouldn't be so lonely like now. With all her heart she wanted to feel like a sister to Miss Carrie again, but she'd given up hope, especially if Miss Carrie's love go to Reverend Mattocks.

Taking a deep breath, Spicey tried to swallow back tears. When thinkin' of being alone, she always got to thinkin' on her mam and pappy. Would her pappy come looking for her one day? When she a chile being tended by Ole Pearl, she remembered breaking a bowl and burying it behind the cabin in her shame. When Ole Pearl asked, "Where de blue bowl?" Spicey lied and said, "I didn't do nuthin'." Her face must a shown her guilt cuz as Ole Pearl turned away, she mumbled under her breath 'bout Spicey being just like her "no-account, lyin' pappy." That the onliest time Spicey heared mention of him.

"You knowed your mammy an' pappy, Betsey?" she asked when Betsey came back to add more warm water.

Betsey's mouth flattened as she dropped her eyes to the soapy water.

A certain stillness came into the room, and Spicey knowed she asked a question that none a her concern. Whether or not Betsey gonna answer, Spicey quick-like cleared her throat and said, "You knowed my mam. Did'cha ever see'd my pappy?"

Betsey went back to her worktable and punched her dough some. "I dun rightly rec'lect yer pappy. They say he here a short spell helpin' with the barrel makin'."

That more than Spicey had heared afore.

Chile-type laughter tinkled in from the yard.

Wiping her hands on her apron, Spicey stepped away for a jiffy to spy on Little Massa Benny and Jess outside. They tossed an egg back and forth, trying not to break it, but they's probably really hoping the other missed the cotch and the egg splat at his feet. She remembered doing the same with Miss Carrie when a chile. Spicey smiled wide.

"Them gowns ain't gonna wash theys'selves," Betsey warned.

Spicey hurried to finish the gown, then rinsed it in another tub of water. Betsey helped her wring it, and Spicey carried it out to hang on the line with the others. Hours later, she finished washing the last gown and, near about nightfall, started in on the ironing. She most times proud of how crisp she could get gowns with the hot iron and a little sprinkle of lavender water, but tonight her arms ached so, and she wished she were anywhere but here.

Later that night in Miss Carrie's bedchamber, Spicey blew the flame out and rushed to her pallet quick-like afore the cold air seeped into her bones. She scootched under the old, thin quilts and gathered them to her real tight, her arms almost too weak to keep them there. One arm cramped some, and she stretched it out under the covers.

November get too frosty in the country. They usually in Swansboro by the end of October, but with Sarah having died, Mistress not ready to move. That is, till Massa Harget come yesterday with the pleasing news of a new grandchile born. Now Mistress wanna go love on that babe. Spicey more than glad to move back into town.

Miss Carrie spent most nights cryin' over Miss Sarah, and tonight no different. She sniffled, and Spicey think on what she gonna say to lull her. Spicey's the onliest one privy to Miss Carrie's frettings and secrets. One of Spicey's duties was to keep Miss Carrie safe—and watching affer her feelings was part of that job. If she sad, Spicey try to make Miss Carrie happy. If she anxious, Spicey remind Miss Carrie of things she can be calm about. Tonight, Spicey ain't doing a good job of keeping Miss Carrie from sorrowing. Spicey mourning right along with Miss Carrie.

"Sarah never have more memories with we'uns, but she be making new memories with angel chilluns. The way I see it, she in a better place where she cain't feel no mo' pain."

Miss Carrie started a cryin' harder, and Spicey thunk maybe she shouldn't have brung to mind the pain Sarah was feeling afore she died. She reached up and found Miss Carrie's hand and held it for a piece, then say, "Wanna pray for comfort?"

"No, Spicey, I don't believe in God anymore." Miss Carrie's voice sounded small, like when she a little girl.

Spicey reckoned she ain't hearing right. "Who we's been praying to all this time, then?"

"I used to think He existed, but if He did, why did he let Sarah die in such a horrible fashion?" Miss Carrie sniffled.

"'Haps He want Sarah safe in the arms of Jesus?"

"You don't know what you're talking about." She growled a little. "I'm tired. Now let me sleep." She pulled her hand outta Spicey's and rolled away.

When Miss Carrie give an order, Spicey knowed best to obey. She thunk on what she could say to her tomorrow night if Miss Carrie still sad. Affer a time, she stopped sniffling, and Spicey reckoned Miss Carrie fell asleep.

Spicey's body ached from all the scrubbing she'd done, but her mind couldn't seem to close-off. Soon she heard fiddling and singing coming from slave row. She heard it many a night since the harvest brought in. The field slaves communed with one 'nuther in ways the house slaves never done. She imagined them laughing and dancing together. Her fists squeezed with envy. What was she missing? She wished they'd invite her to come dancing. She pictured Ezra dancing with some pritty gal.

The whites more Spicey's friends than the blacks, and slavery had no horror for her. Why that be so? Seems lately, even the whites, at least Miss Carrie, not much of a friend. Massa Gibson feel Spicey valuable property—and why he damage his own property? He not. 'Sides, scars on the back only show evidence of a slave to be rebellious, and then he or she won't sell for much.

Massa Gibson feel he gain better results from black drivers like Ezra druther than a white foreman. Spicey always knowed when Ezra 'round cuz he have his eyes on her. Ezra literate and try to command respect of the other slaves. Betsey said this bring in larger crop yields. But she heared the talk from slaves. They not respect Ezra. Could Spicey? Could marrying him and living near the quarter bring her closer to her kind?

She missed her mam's touch and listenin' ear. Mammy the last person to hold Spicey in an embrace and rub her back, soothing her with words only a mam could feel. Spicey sniffled and pushed the memories away. She learned long ago it do no good to linger on 'em.

She thunk again on who she be and what she good for. How she different from some of her own kind. Who would want her and what her future be?

Massa and Mistress say house slaves can help theyselves to the kitchen garden. Those in the quarter has they own plot for a garden. Spicey wouldn't know how to grow nothin'.

The chilluns from the quarter treated special and allowed to pick watermelon in the summer patch. And on Sunday mornings, the house slaves give out biscuits and fruit at the big house. The chilluns line up at the back porch, and Betsey and Cozy dole it on out to 'em. Sometimes Betsey make molasses candy and surprise 'em with a treat. Spicey's favoritest times be when she can serve the chilluns too. They like to play with her—maybe cuz she so small, and they think she's one of 'em. If she make babies with Ezra, mayhap she like having 'em as her own?

But she ain't a field slave. Even though her name Gibson by ownership, she ain't part of the white family either. Who she belong with?

ଓଓଓ

Early, when still dark in the morning, the house slaves get their white folks dressed for traveling. Spicey looked forward to being in town where she could smell the ocean and look out on the sound. Her favoritist reason though was to see her friend Esther. They growed up together, but Esther got taken from Spicey when Miss Julia, now Mistress Harget, marry six years past. Spicey only see Esther at family gatherings and such.

News was Ezra stayin' on the plantation to watch affer its needs. She not sure how she feeling 'bout that. Affer loading the wagons, she see his dark shape against the barn, facing her as they pulled away afore the sun even full up. She imagined his heart sayin' farewell. Thing is, they never said no words to nuther about parting. Wouldn't be right for a fieldhand to approach a house slave for no good reason.

Town be almost a full-day ride. By leaving afore daybreak, they should get there afore supper. The wagons, loaded heavy, make traveling be slow going. Only Massa Gibson was in a buggy at the front. The white folks hoping the house slaves get to town house first to set it up for their liking. They be comin' along at a decent time a day in their carriages, far nuff back to not be in the wagons' dust.

When the sun rose higher, Spicey warmed a bit. Autumn had taken the leaves from the trees. The gray beards of moss still hung from old oak trees, and birds flittin' 'round, looking for they'se morning meal. It pirty country, and no homes in sight.

The wagon hit a rut, and Spicey 'bout tumbled from her perch on the wagon gate. If she plopped off, no one the wiser since they's the last wagon of three and she sat at the end, watching what already passed.

Affer a stop for dinner and watering the horses, they were back on the road for a long spell. She knowed they's close to town when they pass Vinegar Hill, where apple trees growed as far as the eye see. It too late in the season for there to be apples hanging though. Then they passed Horse Heaven. There be a putrid animal carcass rotting in its swampy woods. Spicey pulled her apron over her nose and wiped at watering eyes. The horses pulled the wagon harder and faster, seeming in a hurry to pass on by, maybe knowin' it be one of they own dead out there.

Eventually a gentle, clean breeze rippled at swamp grasses, making 'em sway to a song of croaking frogs. A horse snorted, and the wagon groaned as they started the pull up a rise to Swansboro.

Spicey bent 'round and strained her neck to see the Gibson house on the hill. White homes lined the street all the way down to the waterfront, where water sparkled in small waves and fishing boats rested for the day. Spicey had been told there be ocean just out past where she couldn't see. She'd never see'd it—onliest heared tell of its big waves that pounded the beach.

The air smelled of fish and salt. She sighed, happy to be where she knowed Miss Carrie felt most at home. Might could the move cheer her some? Already Spicey felt better.

The wagon wheels crunched over oyster shells, then the wagon pulled 'round the house and back to the stables.

Spicey jumped down and started unloading the trunks of clothing, anxious to prepare Miss Carrie's bedchamber for her.

CHAPTER ELEVEN

November 23, 1859
White Oak Plantation to Swansboro

Papa had been right. As soon as the news came that Julia gave birth, Mama decided it was time to move into town. The morning of their departure had been a flurry of activity. Three wagons with kitchen goods, clothing, and house slaves left before sunup to prepare the Swansboro house for the family's return.

Caroline's nineteenth birthday had apparently been forgotten. But she didn't feel much like celebrating. In their family, birthdays were usually acknowledged with a butter spice cake or some other sweet. But they were still in mourning and Caroline assumed Mama thought it inappropriate to have any merrymaking because she hadn't recognized the occasion. No one had. In Caroline's reticence, she would not remind them.

At sunrise, Mama, Hester and Benny rode in the buggy driven by Big George, followed by a wagon full of household goods driven by the farmhand slave, Joe, with Caroline by his side. Although over a twenty-mile ride from the plantation to Swansboro, the day was pleasant.

After passing through woods of southern pines and then large, bare oaks draped with gray Spanish moss, they traveled passed harvested and forlorn fields. Morning frost had melted from the woody stalks. The sun warmed the wet earth. A flock of geese ascended through the cloudless, dark blue sky.

Caroline breathed deeply of the earthy fragrance of wet soil.

Before leaving, Mama had reminded Caroline, "Other than giving commands, conversing with a male slave is inappropriate." Consequently, there was little sound other than the wagon's creaks and an occasional honk from high-flying geese. It wasn't like Caroline would've chatted with the slave anyway.

She spent her time dreaming of John and what it would be like for him to court her. She played over and over in her mind how it felt to be in his embrace. Did he actually like her? He'd once told her he admired her strength of character, but did that mean he could care for her as she did for him?

After a taxing day, shadows stretched long. She clasped and unclasped her gloved hands, anxious to be in Swansboro for good and closer to John. She knew the landmarks well and was aware when they neared the town. Apple trees sprinkled the landscape of Vinegar Hill. The gentle wind brought the tang of the salty ocean air.

A wheel slipped into a rut on the dirt road shifting contents of the wagon bed. The lumbering horses didn't hesitate in their pull toward home, but Caroline grabbed the side rail to avoid falling against Joe.

The inlet sound came into view, with a busy late afternoon out on the water. Schooners with full white sails came and went—most bringing supplies for Swansboro's residents and leaving with stores of turpentine in barrels. Sprinkled amongst the schooners, fishing and crabbing boats returned home for the day. The shouts from the fishermen and those on shore to unload their catch were familiar and comforting.

Caroline was thrilled to be back in town where she could enjoy the luxuries of the ocean, which abounded in all kinds of fish, oysters, and crabs. Captivated by the water and busyness of Swansboro, she smiled. She knew most people they passed and shyly waved a greeting.

"Welcome home," called an old friend, Juju, from school.

The carriage stopped in front of Gibson House. Her family alighted.

Papa, who'd traveled ahead with the slaves early that morning, stepped out of the house and waved a welcome to his arriving family.

Caroline's wagon pulled up behind the buggy and stopped.

Joe jumped down and offered his hand.

His open palm gave her pause. She seldom touched a black man. She took his hand but was happy to release it as soon as she stepped onto the crushed oyster shells covering the road. "Thank you, Joe."

"Miz Caroline." His voice deep and quiet, he tilted his head, the ridges of his tribal scars more evident.

She bit her lip and scolded herself for being silly. After all, Spicey touched Caroline all the time, and she never thought a thing of it. And of course, Mammy Abby had cradled Caroline as a babe, caring for her until two years ago when Mammy had died. Their touches were something Caroline had grown used to. It had become the natural way of things.

Mama and Hester disappeared into the house. Benny hung on Papa's arm, but Papa looked pointedly at Caroline. He had a funny grin on his face—the kind someone has when they knew something you didn't. As she walked up the steps and drew near, Benny ran into the house.

"Happy birthday." Papa brought her to him, his coat rough on her cheek, but she felt secure in his embrace.

"Thank you, Papa. Coming to Swansboro is the best present you could give me."

"I think I have one better." Papa released her and the warmth of his smile washed over her like summer rain.

She caught her breath. Maybe life would come back as it used to be. It'd been months since she'd taken walks with Hester or played checkers with Benny. They could do all that here. "What do you mean? Did you get me a present?" She smiled to match his.

"I know it's your nineteenth birthday and not your wedding day, darlin', but I felt the family needed something to lift our spirits." His laughter was a gift. She needed no other. "Like a little music, perchance?" He chuckled again.

It couldn't be. Her eyes grew wide. "Papa . . . you mean I get it now?"

His laughter brought Mama and the others back to the door.

"You'll want it in your own home someday. In the meantime, I can enjoy the music you will bring to ours."

"Where is it, Papa?" Astonished, she walked swiftly into the house passed her family.

"In the parlor," he called.

A few steps down the wide hallway, she entered the room to the left, and there against the wall stood a new square grand piano. "Oh!" She thought it the most delightful thing she'd ever seen.

She ran her hand across its polished surface. The wood felt as smooth as a wakeless sea. The dark brown grain had lovely swirls and lines running along the length of the instrument. The intricate wooden lattice music rack had been set upright, waiting to hold her music. The legs of the piano were as round as barrels but ornately carved. Across the front the maker's names, Hallet and Davis, were embossed in gold. Never had Caroline beheld such an opulent piano. And to think it was hers to keep.

Her family followed her into the parlor.

Benny ran up to the piano. "Thunderation, Carrie, but that's a fine piano."

"Yes, it is." She laughed and went to her father, hugging him firmly. "Thank you kindly, Papa."

"You're most welcome. I purchased it in Boston when I bought the others," he said, referring to the pianos he'd given to her sisters on their wedding days. "Mister Littleton came and tuned it this afternoon. It's been in storage a mighty long time and held up well, has it not?"

"Yes, Papa, it's divine."

He turned toward Mama. "Let's find our Carrie some sheet music."

CHAPTER TWELVE

The day almost gone, amber light filtered through lace window curtains. Caroline perched on her new piano stool, her fingers constantly in motion on the keys as the melodies she played filled the house and vibrated the floorboards to the rooms above. She hoped the melodic notes soothed and lifted her family. She remembered Mama once sharing how herbs had power to heal the body, but it was music that healed the soul.

Caroline's family had long left her alone in the parlor. Surprisingly, they hadn't called her to help unpack. Pushing the sheet music aside, she played memorized pieces she cherished, her long fingers fluidly pressing the keys as the notes told a story without words—the words that always seemed hard for her to express. A change of rhythm gave pleasure to the story, a familiar chorus gave consistency. Moving to the lower keys, she added intensity and conviction, coming somewhere in the middle to find calm and serenity.

Cognizant of a noise behind her, she expected someone had finally come to fetch her, so she brought her music to a finale. She took the slower rhythms and built them to a crescendo, bringing passion to her story. When she finished, the notes vibrated on.

She turned, the round piano stool under her full black mourning skirts pivoting with her, and she gasped.

John stepped further into the parlor.

Her face flushed with warmth. How long had he been listening?

His own face colored as he said, "Sorry to startle you. That was beautiful. I'd love to have you accompany hymns at church sometime."

"Oh, I couldn't do that." Her face grew hotter at the thought of playing in front of John and a congregation. "I'm really not that advanced. I need more practice."

"You're being too modest." He came closer and reached out his hand.

She accepted and stood.

Not in his usual black wool clerical garb, he wore a loose muslin shirt with brown breeches instead. He smelled of lye soap and an unknown fragrance which intrigued her. It reminded her of the smell of the woods after it rained.

He smiled and asked, "Shall we sit for a moment?"

Having John close and still feeling the resonance of the piano crescendo, her heart thudded a little faster than normal. She took a deep breath before answering, "Of course."

As they walked toward the settee, he released her hand. She rubbed her palms along the sides of her skirt to stop the trembling. As she sat, she realized John's grin hadn't left his face. It made her smile too. A quick memory of the week before when he held her in his arms warmed her. Embarrassed, she looked down at the floral pattern of the settee.

John settled next to her. The setting sun filtered through the sheer lace curtains and threw a soft, dappled light across his arm and lap. "I've come from speaking with your father. He's granted me the privilege of courting you."

Caroline tried to keep from showing shock. She hadn't realized John was as interested in her as she was in him even though she'd certainly hoped so. Dazed by the revelation, she didn't know the appropriate thing to say.

"How do you feel about allowing me to court you?" His smile changed to a lopsided grin, leaving him with one dimple instead of two.

Before she could answer, he took her hand in his again, and she examined their clasped fingers. His manicured nails and clean hands were not like the planters she knew well. His skin was smooth. This was a man who read books and harvested a different kind of field.

She avoided looking into his discerning eyes. "You've taken me unexpected like. I didn't know you felt . . . well." She swallowed and shifted; her heavy black mourning skirts crinkled. The hoops made them sit high above her knees. In her nervousness, she let go of his hand to straighten her skirts.

He cleared his throat and put his hand on his lap, his expression confused. "Our last meeting at the church took me quite by surprise, and I seem to be able to envision little else."

Delighted at his admission, she thought again of being in his arms. "I'm a bit embarrassed for being so overwrought when last we met. Do forgive my weaknesses."

John gently tilted her chin. "There's nothing to forgive. I'm touched you came to me with your sorrows." His sincere brown eyes, as dark as the blackwater river nearby, matched the truth of his words. "I've always been impressed with your compassion toward your family. Even before Sarah's death, you've been the quiet peacemaker."

The kindness of his compliment drew her to him. He'd paid closer attention to their previous conversations than she'd realized. "You did bring immense comfort to me the other day . . . in the church." Her mouth quirked upward. "Thank you, kindly."

His face became serious, both dimples now gone. "I perhaps overstepped propriety, do forgive me. You came to me for comfort, and I took you in my arms because of my own desires not just to comfort, but to be closer to you. Will you forgive me?"

Caroline wanted to tell him she liked his embrace, but such words shouldn't be uttered by a lady. "There's nothing to forgive. You made me feel happier than I have in months." Her words sounded more forward than she'd anticipated, but they brought back his dimples, and she didn't regret her honesty.

Without taking his eyes from hers, he took her hand again. The gesture completely natural. "I'm pleased." He grinned broadly, his straight teeth as lovely as his dimples.

Her contentedness helped her relax. It was marvelous sitting close to him. Touching him.

His expression became grave. "It's burdened my soul to hear of your unhappiness, and to see the suffering brought upon you by your sister's passing."

"I want the pain to go away." Caroline wasn't sure how to react at hearing him tell her he cared about her suffering. "I need to help my family feel happiness again. Being in Swansboro may help the burden become lighter." Telling him her concerns came easy, as usual, so unlike sharing feelings with anyone else. It had always been so with John.

"I'm gratified to hear it. Since we met last week, I've been employed on a sermon about overcoming sorrow."

"You're qualified to give such a sermon." Caroline responded, struck by John's thoughtfulness.

He gave a slight twitch of his shoulder, as if he wasn't sure of his abilities. "I pray I am. I'll try to be sensitive to your feelings."

"I'll encourage my family to come to the service."

What she saw in his eyes moved her. He gazed at her with what she could only describe as joy. Feeling self-conscious of his gaze and what it might mean, she peered through the lace curtains. The sun was almost down. Cozy would be in soon to light the lamps.

"You haven't answered my question. I'd very much like to court you." His face earnest, his eyes warmed with affection.

"I'm sorry I ever let you consider I wouldn't. I'd very much like to be courted by you." To convince him of her words she daringly gave his hand a slight squeeze. "I look forward to spending time together. If you're sure I'm worthy."

A look of surprise came over his face. "Are you speaking of the faith you questioned at our last encounter?"

"Yes." She squirmed, then boldly rubbed her thumb along his index finger, immediately regretting the action. It wasn't right to be so forward with a man of God. "I'm not sure I'm befitting for a preacher . . . especially you. You're the most upright person I know."

"Please don't consider those foolish notions. As we've discussed the gospel in the past, I've been impressed by your understanding and strength of character. I know it's new to you, but your curiosity will be your virtue." His eyes pinched in worry. "I'm a believer in following God's ways. Does that make you uncomfortable?"

She feared John could see into her soul. His question had to be answered, even if she wasn't sure of the answer herself. She tried to respond as honestly as possible. "I admire your faith. But what will you think if I can never be as worthy of God's love as you?"

John briefly glanced toward the window. The dying sun highlighted his cheek bones. She'd never seen him with whiskers, which many men his age wore. His face—clean of hair—somehow made him appear to be more pure than other men. She wanted to touch his cheek.

"I find myself drawn to you." He turned to her. "I'm sure the feelings I have are accepted by God. God loves us all the same, Caroline. I'm not favored."

She wasn't sure she believed him *not favored*, but she did like that he was drawn to her. Would he eventually find her naive about spiritual matters? She couldn't understand why he had interest in her, but she promptly decided she didn't need to understand his reasons. She'd follow her heart and desires, and those feelings were for John. "Well, then God has shown *me* favor." She straightened. "I'll try not to disappoint either of you."

With his free hand he briefly rubbed her upper arm, then just as quickly dropped it to his side, his neck reddening.

Touching each other was new to both of them. Caroline lowered her eyes.

His shirt was clean and newly pressed, probably having been recently whitened by the sun. Still holding his left hand, she boldly reached for his right, and he willingly grasped hers. "People will be watching us," she said with concern. "They'll expect more than I'm afraid I can fulfill."

He smiled a kind of silly smile, like he would at a child who was caught stealing a cookie. "Why would you think that? In truth, people will wonder how I was lucky enough to gain your affections."

"You're always so kind." She tilted her head. "What person wouldn't want to be with you?"

It was a question she didn't expect him to answer, but he did in mock seriousness. "Too many, I'm afraid, but I'm working on them."

She laughed, knowing he was referring to those not in his congregation. In all the time she'd known him, it was the first jest she'd heard from his lips. A weight lifted from her shoulders. She was content, a feeling she'd been wanting for months. "Will you stay for supper?"

"I'd love to."

"It's my birthday. Did you know?"

"I had no idea." His eyes lit. "I'm glad I came on such a special day. Forgive me for having no gift."

"You being here is gift enough."

CHAPTER THIRTEEN

That evening, as Caroline's family and John sat at the supper table and ate, her senses were heightened with John next to her. She noticed every move he made and every expression that crossed his face. He had the manners of a gentleman.

Papa spoke to him about farming, slavery, and the news of John Brown at Harper's Ferry. John politely added to the conversation. Caroline was glad he hadn't worn his clergyman's garb, hoping the absence of it helped Papa warm to him.

"What happened to the blackies you inherited from your father's estate when you turned eighteen?" Papa asked John.

"Out of state. I lost track of them when I left the country in '56 to travel to Jerusalem." John looked to his plate.

Lost track of them? An unusual answer. She'd heard rumors he objected to slavery and she never wanted to discuss the issue. Papa would disapprove if the rumors were true.

Papa took a bite of ham. "I heard you went to Jerusalem. What got in your head to go there?"

John didn't seem to notice the derision.

But Caroline shifted in her seat. Papa could've phrased the question with less condescension. She'd learned during earlier conversations that talking about Israel and the Hebrews was one of John's favorite subjects.

Sitting up straighter, he became animated, passion evident in his eyes. "I read the *Works of Josephus* when I was fifteen and again at seventeen. The history of the Jews is fascinating."

Papa stared at John as if he'd said his dog had birthed kittens.

Caroline put her napkin to her mouth to hide her grin, but Hester couldn't quite stifle her giggle.

Mama flashed a disappointed look in Hester's direction and cleared her throat. "I've never heard of the book, Reverend Mattocks, but it must be quite interesting. As you've probably noted, there's been talk in my family that my Simmons ancestors were Hebrew. I know nothing about them." She simpered. "I guess we just don't know what we'll find in our family tree."

"We learn in the Bible the Jews were God's chosen people." John addressed Mama. "I went to Israel to try to understand why."

Papa remained suspiciously quiet, then stifled a yawn.

"Did you get any answers?" Always the hostess, Mama carried polite conversation.

Caroline doubted she wanted to know the answer. She glanced at Hester, who rolled her eyes.

John set down his fork and leaned back in his chair. "It's still somewhat of a mystery to me, but I believe God will someday reveal His mysteries. I found the Jews to be strict in their observance of the Sabbath day and many other laws and commandments. I'm now in the process of studying the Torah, which is similar to our Old Testament."

Alarm flew over Mama's face and her eyebrows shot up. "You don't find it sacrilege to read another religion's scripture?"

Caroline clenched her jaw. Wanting her family to like John, she worried their lack of religious understanding might cause division.

Calmly, John displayed his usual seriousness. "The Jewish people follow an Abrahamic religion, as do we."

Caroline swallowed. Benny swirled mashed potatoes around on his plate, obviously bored with the conversation. Hester markedly stared at Caroline, having told her earlier that she thought Caroline's taste in beaus was poor, silently judging John as boring and stuffy. The look on Hester's face was full of, *I told you so*. Caroline scowled at her sister and turned to give John her full attention.

Papa cleared his throat. "Well John, I hear your brother Kit is being learned in the way of doctoring, like your stepfather." Papa had no doubt become impatient with subjects he didn't understand, much less thought anyone should take the time to study.

"Yes, he is." If John was disappointed in the change of subject, he was polite enough not to show discontent. "I'm sure he'll make a fine doctor. Mother has said if I cannot heal someone with prayer, perhaps Kit can heal them with his doctoring. I believe she's hoping we'll be able to keep the whole town alive for many years to come."

They all laughed, and Caroline almost choked on her food. Before this day, she'd never heard John tell a joke, and now he'd told two. Maybe she didn't know him so well after all. But she wanted to.

"Modern medicine can work miracles," Papa said.

Caroline stiffened and took a quick sideways glance at John. She thought Papa's comment a slight to John's faith, but she kept her judgement to herself.

"God's miracles are greater than any medicine," Mama said. Her thoughts must've been running along the same vein as Caroline's.

"We should all believe in miracles. We can give thanks to God for the miracle of medicine." John turned to Mama. "And medicinal herbs." Typical of John to bring peace to the conversation.

Benny squirmed in his seat. "When will Betsey serve Carrie's birthday cake?"

Mama looked to Zylphia standing near the door that led through a covered passageway to the cookhouse. With a nod from Mama, Zylphia disappeared and came back with Betsey and Cozy. From the sideboard they removed the still generously full platters of ham, lobster, potatoes, and dishes of seasoned vegetables and gravy.

The solemn ritual of toting food away went on as it did each night. Caroline was more aware than usual of how finely dressed the slaves appeared and whether they performed their duties courteously as expected. She wanted John to be impressed by the Gibson affluence.

Betsey came into the room with a look of delight directed at Caroline. She carried a two-layered spice cake with a shiny honey glaze dripping down the sides. Following her, Zylphia bore a silver tray with goblets and a carafe of scuppernong wine.

John's hand brushed Caroline's under the table. Whether intentional or not, the sensation moved through her body.

"Happy birthday, Carrie," her family chorused.

"And may there by many more." John smiled warmly.

She perhaps gazed at his lips a little too long. Everyone's eyes were on her, and she assumed they saw the look that passed between her and John. A hot flush went up her neck onto her cheeks. To avoid more embarrassment, she turned to watch Betsey place the cake on the sideboard.

Betsey cut the cake with their best silver server. The confection smelled of sweet apples and cinnamon—the aroma of comfort.

Once everyone had been served, Betsey left, and Zylphia resumed her station by the door, looking at the wall opposite her, but with Mama in her peripheral vision. The large silver candelabra in the center of the table created a warm, contented light.

Papa poured wine into a crystal goblet and passed it to Caroline at his right. She handed it to John, showing honor to serve the guest first. Papa filled the goblets and passed them until everyone had their own. In Benny's, he poured only an inch of wine and added water to fill the glass full.

Papa held his goblet in front of him, looking into the deep purple of the wine. "To my lovely daughter, Caroline." He paused as if his throat caught.

Surprised at his sudden sentimentality, Caroline worried about his fragility so soon after losing a daughter. A warm and generous man with his family, but never with strangers, she was bewildered he allowed his emotions to show in front of John.

"Because of the recent loss of one . . ." Papa cleared his throat. "I'm reminded how precious my children are to me." He looked up to the ceiling as if in supplication. "You are all a gift to me." He then glanced around at their faces. "We have shared in our suffering."

Mama sat motionless, gaze fixed on the tablecloth.

"But we must remember to rejoice in what we do have." Papa forced a smile and gazed at Caroline. "I adore you, little lamb!" He raised his glass high, as did everyone but Caroline. "To Caroline," he said, and all repeated the words and sipped from their glasses.

John whispered, "Amen," as if Papa had uttered a prayer.

No one else heard him, and it puzzled her, but there was no time to think on it because she was expected to show her gratitude, which she humbly did.

Later that evening, after a game of cribbage, John gave his thanks and announced his intentions to leave. Hester was given the eye by Mama, who followed John and Caroline out onto the porch.

John's hands hung down as if he didn't know what to do with them. "Thank you for a delightful evening."

He was much too close to her. Feeling conscious of their chaperone, she looked away before she got lost in his intense eyes and forgot herself. Having him so near pricked every nerve. "I've enjoyed our visit and hope to see you again soon."

"You will." He lifted her gloved hand and, at the last minute, turned it upward and placed a soft kiss on her bare wrist.

Caroline gasped.

Hester giggled.

"Happy birthday, Caroline," he said as he walked down the steps out onto Elm Street.

Caroline stood as if frozen, although she was much too warm to be cold. She watched him until the night took him home.

"Carrie, perhaps your preacher isn't so divine after all." Hester laughed all the way into the house and down the hall.

Caroline had to disagree.

CHAPTER FOURTEEN

November 27, 1859

On Sunday, Spicey met Esther out front a the Harget home and moseyed arm-in-arm downhill toward the water.

Massa and Mistress Harget had a town house in Swansboro and a plantation in the country, same as Massa Gibson. The Gibson and Harget two white town homes, with piazzas on all sides, stand three-stories tall across Main Street from each other. When both families in town for winter, Spicey visited with Esther some.

"My chile Lemmy died a malaria since I see'd ya last," Esther wiped at a tear and took a deep breath. "But I have 'nuther boy chile. Charlie and me name him Joey." She gaze far off, toward the pier, where nets had been draped to dry and fishing boats be moored, waiting for Monday and the weeks' work.

Esther continued in her bold way of talk. "Mistress Julia gave Joey to her plantation fieldslave while he still at my breast, jus' like she done wid Nellie, so's da babe not hin'rance wid my work for her. Charlie send word when he can on how Nellie and Joey doin' at the plantation."

Esther stepped away and turned to Spicey, and where Spicey think she gonna see sorrow, she see fire. Esther's jawline jut out even more than usual, and she squinted her droopy eyes. "I spoke wid de root doctor 'bout my future, and she tole me I be free somedee. She gave me a conjurin' charm."

Long as Spicey knowed Esther, she always dreamed 'bout freedom. She little more than three years older than Spicey and already have three chilluns—one now dead. Spicey 'spected she needed a sense of control where they is none. Esther always wanted to get back at Mistress Harget for something.

Esther was loud and bold with her talk, but Spicey lean in to whisper, "You gonna leave your chilluns behind when you git your freedom?"

"Course not. I find a way ta git 'em." She pushed out her lip. "I hopin' what comes 'round goes 'round. Some a us helpin' a runaway who escaped for a second time. She say she knows you."

That stopped Spicey in her steps. "Who that be?"

"A black girl who looks white. Annie Mae be her name."

Hope surged in Spicey, and she clutched her hands at her chest. Annie Mae be alive! "Where she be?"

"She move 'round some, near about town outskirts. Ya know anyone who can git her north?"

No one. Spicey lowered her head. "Nah. What to do?"

"Spicey."

Spicey knowed Miss Carrie's voice anywhere and turned to see her on the arm of Reverend Mattocks, and Spicey's heart dropped some to see the two together like that. Miss Carrie far nuff away to've not heared Esther and her talk. "Yessum?" she call.

"You come on home now, here. I need to change for supper."

"Yessum." It 'spose to be her day off, but never there be a day off from dressing the white womenfolk. They couldn't do it they'selves with those corsets and crinolines and such. Spicey nodded her farewell to Esther. "I'll be seeing you next week."

She hurried toward Gibson House. As she passed the couple, she heared Miss Carrie say to her man, "I wouldn't know what to do without Spicey. No one has a better servant."

He looked like he thunk on it some but didn't comment back. The rumor was, he with the black folk.

CHAPTER FIFTEEN

December 4, 1859

On Sundays, Miss Carrie never call Spicey until Miss Carrie needed help changing for bed, so that night Spicey hid near the front porch of Gibson House, waiting for the reverend to leave.

It chilly, and she wonderin' how Annie Mae get on in that old boathouse down passed Pickett's Bay where Spicey sneak Annie Mae a few days back. Spicey saw plenty of fishnets piled inside. 'Haps Annie Mae hunker down under 'em to keep warm.

Spicey been keeping an eye on Reverend Mattocks all week, watching for signs of his feelings toward the black folks. He look 'em in the eye and treat 'em with proper manners, but still she couldn't tell if he be for their freedom. If he believe what he preach 'bout 'love thy neighbor' and 'do unto others as you'd have 'em do unto you,' then she think he might help some with Annie Mae.

Standing at the corner of the house, Spicey got a blast of cold coming up off the river. She needed to get Annie Mae somewhere warm and safe—and soon. She pulled her quilt tighter around herself. Her ears and nose be chilled, but she not yet cold enough to give up and go inside.

The candlelight shining through a nearby winduh attracted a moth. *Tap, tap, tap.* It fluttered against the glass. Waves lapped the shores far below, and the smell of the boggy mud lining the shoreline of White Oak River drifted up on the breeze. It weren't somethin' she liked to be smellin'. Too fishy.

Finally, someone step out, and it be Reverend Mattocks, Miss Carrie, and Miss Hester.

"Thank you for a lovely evening, Caroline. I hope to see you again soon," he say in his deep, smooth voice.

Miss Carrie laugh a little nervous like. What make her nervous 'round such a nice man of God?

Spicey shook her head for her dotty Miss.

Miss Hester glance about, then look Spicey's way.

Spicey quick-like sink back further into darkness, not able to hear Miss Carrie's answer. For not the first time, Spicey ax'd herself where her loyalties lie. If she want bad to be family with Miss Carrie, why sneak 'round and risk her position by helpin' Annie Mae?

Soon she heard the reverend's deep voice say his farewells and footsteps crunch across Main Street. Spicey peek 'round the corner and see the last of Miss Carrie's skirts as they sweep into Gibson House. Spicey dropped her quilt since it brighter than the black dress she have on and hurry through the darkness affer Reverend Mattocks, her heart beatin' like a wild animal tryin' to escape her chest.

As he travel down Elm Street, he must've heared her comin' for he stopped and turned, a crease to his brow. "Who goes there?"

Spicey come close so's he sees her. "It's Spicey, Massa Mattocks."

"No need to call me Massa, Spicey," he said.

Spicey believe she made a wise choice to talk to him.

"Has Miss Caroline sent you with a message?"

"Nah, Massa . . . I mean, Reverend." Spicey swallow hard, trying to remember the speech she'd been preparing.

"What is it then?" he said real gentle like, trying to coax her talk.

Spicey looked to the dark porches lining the road, making sure no one about. She whispered, "Do men of God help *all* in need?" She wrapped her arms around herself, more to hold in her quaking than from the cold. She risked a lot talking to a white man about a runaway slave. She could get sold away and Annie Mae caught in the end. *Please, Lord, help me know words to say.*

Reverend Mattocks smiled, and Spicey understand why Miss Carrie always going on 'bout his dimples and all. He a handsome man that make Spicey feel a little tingly herself.

"I'd like to think so. Do you know someone in need? Can I help this person?" His brown eyes creased in curiosity but also kindness.

Spicey drew in a deep breath, closed her eyes, and silently shouted to the Lord one more time for His direction, then asked Reverend, "You help runaway slaves?"

Reverend not flinch or narrow his eyes or scowl. He look 'round hisself, then slowly nod. "Why did you think to come to me?"

"Rumor among nigras, you have symp'thies." She watched him closely, feeling more relaxed all the while. She could sense his kind heart, and she finally sure she not wrong in coming to him.

"Walk with me," he said.

They walked down dark Elm Street, the moon hid behind clouds. The crunching muffled their words as Spicey told him about Annie Mae and where she hiding.

"There's a network of sympathetic watermen assisting those desiring freedom," he said, his big words sounding intelligent and in control of how things stack up. "We must get her to the Neuse River near New Bern."

"How we do that?"

"I have a man who helps. I can't take slaves there in conveyances regularly or the authorities will figure out my involvement. In the dark of night, my man sneaks them there. You must take us to where your friend is hiding, and he'll help her from there." He glanced sidelong at her. "When can we do that?"

"I fear the cold weather kill her soon. I can sneak out any night affer I put My Miss to bed." What he think a her sneaking out? Did he see it as a deceit against the woman he courtin'? "How soon you help?" she asked before he make comment.

He hummed a bit under his breath. "The man who helps me is a slave."

Spicey sucked in a surprised gasp.

"I'll speak with him and somehow get a message to you. Let us try and do it this week . . . maybe toward the end of the week?"

Relief brought tears to Spicey's eyes. She wiped at them. "Oh, much obliged," was all she could say. For the first time, she felt hope that Annie Mae could truly find freedom and, most importantly, safety.

As Spicey ran home, it dawned on her that she'd put safety as more necessary than freedom.

CHAPTER SIXTEEN

December 8, 1859

Shakin' like a leaf barely hangin' onto its branch, Spicey crept 'round trees along the swampy edge of Frog Pond. It smelled as bad as the chamber pots she emptied each day. She pulled her shawl over her nose. Stepping as quick as she dared through the muck without making noises louder than the frogs, she hoped she not tote home the smell on her shoes. Problem be, the nearby frogs stop croakin' when she slog on by. But by the grace of God, the inky darkness held thick clouds covering a half moon. She prayed no one see her in black clothes.

"Keep me safe, Mammy," she whispered, calling out from her heart to her dead mam, like she always done when afeared.

She knowed she must be late. Miss Carrie hadn't fallen asleep until affer she'd talked about Reverend Mattocks until the clock struck more dongs than Spicey could count. Thereupon, Spicey had to skedaddle—while staying out of sight off the road—lumbering to Horse Heaven, to the meeting place Reverend Mattocks told her 'bout.

She heared a noise and stopped dead still, listening. The frogs quieted too. Affer a moment, they start their song, and she thunk no man near. She peered about, seeing nothin' but blackness all 'round. Mayhap a nighthawk took flight. She waited until her heart slowed before moving on.

Tain't like when she helped Annie Mae in the country. If Spicey caught here, there no explaining why she away from home. The paddy rollers traveling the road think she a runaway, for sure.

She found Reverend Mattocks sitting real quiet on a wagon seat, off the road in a thick knot of trees. "Massa . . ." she called in a holler-whisper and then cleared her throat, correcting herself.

"Reverend," she said a bit louder as she stepped to the wagon, not wanting to alarm him with her coming.

He smiled wide, his white teeth about all she see'd in the darkness. "I was worried you weren't coming."

Thinking her Miss not want her sharing the truth of why she late, she said, "I never give up on helpin' Annie Mae."

He bent down and gave her a hand up onto the wagon seat.

"You want me in back?" She never rode in the front afore.

"That would be best, if you don't mind."

Never having had a white man be considerate of her feelings, she had to give his face a second look to make sure he ain't foolin' with his manners. His smile show he ain't.

"Slip on back there." He turned his head to the opening in the canvas. "Junior, give her a hand if you don't mind."

There he go with his *don't mind* again. And who he talkin' to?

A large, black hand, pale palm up, reach out a the wagon-cover opening.

Spicey hesitantly placed her small hand inside his. Although a cold night, the hand be warm, sending alarming heat to Spicey's bosom. Catching her breath, she climbed on back, and his other hand came to her waist, guiding her to a hay bale where she plopped down.

The space in almost complete blackness, Spicey could barely make out a man so tall, even when sitting, his head almost touched the canvas top. The whites of his eyes large and slanted to kindness.

"How do," he said with a voice like two drumbeats.

The wagon moved a jolt, and Spicey grabbed at the bale before fallin' against the man's knees. Once on the road, she finally let out the breath she'd been holding. Her body trembled more than it had sneakin' to the meeting spot. "I don't rightly know." Now why she sound like her Miss? She bit her lip. "I never free a slave afore. I 'spect you be Reverend Mattocks's slave who help him with such?"

"My massa his brother, Kit Mattocks. Reverend ain't have no slaves."

"His brother know you here?"

"He do." Two more drumbeats.

"Why your massa have slaves but help others git away?"

"Complicated," the deep voice said.

She searched her memory for this man's name. "'Scus'm, but what your name?"

"I Junior Mattocks. My family been wid Mattocks owners long afore I can remembra."

"They *your* family?"

"Whatcha mean?" Without seeing his face clearly, she still knowed he frowned.

Spicey wasn't sure how to answer. She confused where her ties should be knotted. The Gibsons the onliest family she know. "My mammy die, and I have no brothers or sisters. My pappy may someday come back."

"Your pappy a slave?"

"Believe so."

"Where he?"

"Don't know. Never met him."

"He know you exist?"

The question hit Spicey in the heart like he'd thrown a spear. She held back a whimper. "Don't know."

Junior harrumphed. "White folk ain't never gonna be yer kin."

Spicey jammed back hard, trying to control hurt feelings. Junior remind her of what she knowed but didn't want to think on.

The wagon rocked as they traveled toward White Oak River. The wheel on Spicey's side squeaked its way 'round. She pulled her shawl up onto her neck and tucked loose curls behind a scrap of fabric she'd tied on her head before leaving Gibson House. Although her body had stopped quivering, her hands still shook, and her breath came fast.

Junior's breathing stayed slow and steady. He seemed used to traveling at night to help slaves. She wondered how many times he'd done this afore.

His steadiness calmed her some. And knowing she with a white man who could pose as her massa, make her hope all be well. She looked to Junior's dark figure. "If you help slaves escape, why you still here? Sounds like you know how to gain freedom."

"I can do more for my people by stayin' here. 'Sides, I'm in good standin' with Massa Kit. I growed up wid him as my friend, and he still treat me as such."

Spicey wished Miss Carrie still did.

Junior grunted. "If I left, I'd have ta take my whole family wid me so's I wouldn't be alone. How we fit us hidden in a wagon or bound on a ship? Wouldn't be worth leavin' if I alone."

"How big your family?" Envy tightened Spicey's fists.

"Mam, Pappy, twin sister, and brudder older dan me, one brudder come affer me."

"Oh," Spicey squeak out. Junior had what she'd always dreamed of. "You blessed."

He quiet for a spell then said, "I unnerstan yer loyalty to yer white owners." He touched her hand.

She pulled away as if he fire.

"But dey ain't never gonna be *yer* kin," he said again.

Who I have then?

The wagon tilted downward. Spicey peeked out the back. They'd left the road. She could smell the rottenness of the river's low-lying bog. They at the swampy area by the salt marsh—the place Spicey had to cross to get Annie Mae hidden.

Reverend Mattocks clicked to the horses to get them to giddyap, but they go even slower.

"Mud," Junior say.

"Whoa," Reverend Mattocks give the command and then turn to the canvas opening. "This is as far as I dare go without getting stuck."

Junior leave the wagon from the back and lower the tail. "Lemme he'p ya down," he said to Spicey.

The rising heat of a blush flustered her as she moved to the back of the wagon.

Junior placed both hands on her waist, lifting her like she no more than a sack of grain. He set her solid on her feet, but she tottered in nervousness like waves pitching her off balance.

He moved real quick to catch her 'round the shoulders. He smelled like hay and man. The smell of hard work.

She never smelled nothin' like him afore and wanted to take a deeper breath, but he stepped away.

Reverend Mattocks be by Junior's side. How long he been there? What he see? Spicey swallowed hard.

Junior pulled a bulging knapsack from the wagon.

"Can you take us to Annie Mae from here?" Reverend asked her.

Spicey looked about to get her bearings by judging where the river lie. "We at Pickett's Bay." Spicey pointed upriver. "She this way."

Leading the men, Spicey knowed her strides through the wet and reeking sludge were short. She glad it wasn't summer when bugs bit and stung. She watched for sleeping snakes and gators and hoped the men weren't cross on account she movin' slow. All her senses felt Junior's presence and positions at her side or just behind her.

If they got caught out here, Reverend Mattocks have an excuse of taking his slaves to get an early start on oyster digging. How he explain doing it on such a dark night, she not rightly know.

Coming up to the old boathouse, she paused and pointed at the shoreline by a broken pier. She'd done told Annie Mae the plans earlier in the week and hoped she safe inside. Two big men likely scare her. "Stay here," Spicey said, embarrassed for sounding bossy. "Please . . . if you will." *Just shut your mouth girl.* She rolled her eyes at herself.

The door of the boathouse hung crooked, attached by one hinge. "It me, Annie Mae," she whispered. "You here?" Spicey's heart fluttered fast like bird wings.

A little noise came from inside. Annie Mae peek from the edge of the broken door. "I here. You alone?" Moisture filled the one hazel eye Spicey could see.

"Nah. The mens here to rescue you." Spicey grinned to try and ease Annie Mae's fretting.

"Aw, Lawd," Annie Mae breathe. She shifted the door enough to slide her small body out.

The men came forward, and Annie Mae backed up to Spicey, keeping her eyes on the white reverend. "Ya sure?" she whispered to Spicey from the side of her mouth.

"They's good men. Don't fear none."

Reverend step forward. "I'm Reverend Mattocks." He reached a hand to shake Annie Mae's.

Unsure, she not take it, and he let his drop. "This is Junior. He'll get you through the Croatan forest. The journey will last days, but there aren't many roads through there, and you'll be able to stay hidden. I've arranged safe passage on a vessel waiting for you, anchored on the Neuse River."

Annie Mae kept nodding but said nothin'.

Spicey took the girl's cold hand, and it shook worse than Spicey's. "It be jus' fine," she said.

Annie Mae nodded, her teeth chattering.

Spicey took off her shawl and wrap it 'round Annie Mae.

Junior raised a brow and then stared Spicey in the eye with what look like favor.

Reverend Mattocks stepped closer. "Don't worry, Junior has done this many times before."

Spicey wonder how many. He be right when he said he didn't run affer freedom hisself cuz he could do more for slaves here.

"When the boat docks in Boston, there'll be people waiting for you—to give you a place to live and work to do," Reverend said.

"Thank ya." Annie Mae tried to smile. She turned to Spicey. "I's scared."

Spicey held the girl. She smelled of dried fish, mayhap from the nets. "Be happy. The Lord is watchin' over you. He even sent a reverend and nice black man to undertake your safety." She embraced her tighter. "I loves you."

Annie Mae sniffled, holding on to Spicey. "I loves ya too. I want ya to come wid me."

Why hadn't Spicey thunk of that? She'd never dreamed of her own freedom. Never wanted to leave Miss Carrie. Still didn't. "If I ever git free, I'll come find you."

Pulling away, Annie Mae's hazel eyes shown with hope, and a real smile crept onto her face. "I be waitin'."

She stepped to Junior's side.

He towered over her, and Spicey felt relief that he be Annie Mae's protector.

Reverend Mattocks and Junior had some quiet words, embraced, and then Junior and Annie Mae leave. Spicey glanced back, and felt she'd lost the one hope of a sister. She blinked tears from her eyes.

"We best be on our way," Reverend said.

Before Spicey turned from the two silhouettes walking into deep darkness, a strange feeling came into her heart. *She* wanted to be walking at Junior's side but toward home. Then another thought—what if he like Annie Mae's bewitching eyes? Jealousy steal her hope for Annie Mae for just one moment. Spicey shook her head, clearing the devil sneakin' in. *Git behind me Satan.*

ങങങ

Spicey shivered in the wagon, burrowing into the hay. Eventually, she dozed. Her eyes burst open as she realized sunshine be shimmering on the canvas. She catched her breath. "Sun comin' up Reverend Mattocks," she whispered near the canvas opening.

"I know," he said worried like.

Spicey glance outta the opening and see slaves already entering a field, the houses of Swansboro just coming into view. "Miss Carrie be lookin' for me."

"Let's hope not." His voice strained with the words.

As they near Gibson House, her stomach soured.

Miss Carrie be on the porch, dressed in her black mourning day dress, hems puddling at her feet cuz she have no hoops under. Spicey could tell she slouched some and wearing no corset either. These things Miss need Spicey to help with. Miss Carrie's braids dangling outta a shawl she'd draped over her head, and she lookin' this way and that. As they get closer, Spicey see Miss Carrie's scowl, but as soon as she recognize Reverend Mattocks, that change to surprise, then pleasure, then confusion. She back up into the shadows of the porch.

Spicey know she not want Reverend seeing her undone. Spicey in all kinds of trouble. "What I do?" she whispered.

"Leave it to me," Reverend Mattocks said.

Spicey moved further back in the wagon cover's shadow.

"Good morning, Caroline," he called a greeting and stopped the wagon close to the porch.

She stepped forward. "Well, I'll be, what brings you out so early?"

"I was just going to ask you the same thing."

"My servant appears to be missing." She shrugged. "I've looked everywhere and just stepped out to see if she's out here for some odd reason."

Reverend cleared his throat. "I'd like to talk to you about that."

What he means? Spicey trembled down to her frozen toes.

"Whatever do you mean?" Miss Carrie asked.

"Spicey is with me," he said.

Spicey sucked in a sharp breath.

"She's what?" Misses voice go up higher than a warbler.

CHAPTER SEVENTEEN

Caroline put her hand to her head. "I don't understand." Why would Spicey be with John?

John jumped down from the wagon, disappeared behind it, then stepped into view with Spicey next to him.

"You run and do your chores," he said to her. "I'll explain everything."

As Spicey scampered off toward the back entrance, she kept her eyes to the ground.

Where was her shawl on such a cold day?

Coming up the porch, the look in John's eyes was as if he were contemplating the fate of their future.

Was he? What an odd notion.

She was never good at confrontation, and the last thing she wanted to do was grill John, so she hoped he'd be kind enough to explain. Surely, he wasn't the kind of man to dally with female slaves. She shook her head again, unsure. "Why did you have my slave with you?" Her heart stilled as she waited for the answer.

He took her hand. "You need to know something about me."

She yanked her hand from his and backed away. "Do tell," she said through the tightness of her throat.

He stepped close again and raised her chin so she'd look at him. Her traitorous heart thrilled at his touch.

"I sometimes help slaves gain their freedom," he whispered.

She gasped. "No!" Why did he do such a foolish thing? "Why?" Was he taking Spicey away from her? It made no sense.

He frowned. "Why not?" He dropped his hand, stepping back.

"You've grown up with slaves. They even now work your mother's land, care for her home. It wasn't so long ago you lived there. Why have you made this decision?"

He pushed out a breath and stared down the street. "I've wanted to talk to you about my conflicting lifestyle for some time. It's a dangerous thing I do."

"Dangerous and foolhardy." Wanting to shake him, she clenched her hands instead.

He turned and brought his gaze to her again. "You think me a fool?"

Caroline had the sudden instinct to flee rather than argue. "It's only that you're breaking the law. My papa wouldn't like it either—wouldn't let you court me if he knew."

John nodded. "These are my constant thoughts. What do I give up, my illegal activities or you?"

The way he said *you* held such endearment that tears gathered in her eyes. "Is the answer not clear?" Was he telling her he'd choose freeing slaves over her? She placed her hand on her stomach that suddenly clenched in cold fear.

He raked a hand through his hair. "It's not."

"John," she cried, tears falling.

He stepped close again. "Don't cry. We can work this out." He wiped her tears with both thumbs, holding her face in his hands.

Would his touch be forever a thrill? For a moment she thought he would kiss her, but he frowned instead.

She wanted to believe him—that they would work it out. Could they just pretend this conversation never happened and go about their lives as they had been?

"We both know what it's like to live with slaves. For generations, our families have enslaved peoples. Don't think I don't understand your feelings." He dropped his hands. "I've been praying about it—your and my future. God is good. He'll show me the way."

Hollow inside, she hugged herself. God had never done her any favors. Never talked to her. Never saved her sister. "If we wed, would you free my slaves?"

He shrugged.

"I'll never give up Spicey. And why, by the way, was she with you this morning?"

John hesitated.

Caroline's fear grew colder still. "Will we always have secrets?"

"I don't want it to be so." His brown eyes beseeched her understanding. "Spicey knew where a runaway slave hid and traveled with me to show me the place."

"You're involving my slave in your crimes? Papa will have you arrested!"

John clamped his mouth shut. His jaw clenched.

She suspected he'd not tell her the whole truth. "How can we have a relationship with secrets between us?" she repeated, needing the answer as much as she needed air to breathe.

"We can't," he said simply, but his mouth drew down in sadness.

This could not be happening. The man she'd counted on for easy companionship, loving and kind care, a solid foundation and advice, was telling her they could no longer have a relationship. She swiftly turned to leave.

John didn't call her back.

ೂ⊰⊱ೂ

Caroline had run away yet again. Why hadn't she stayed to work things out? Stepping into her bedchamber, she found Spicey with her back to a recently stoked fire, holding Caroline's brush. "I'm here for your morning ministrations," Spicey said meekly.

"How could you, Spicey!" Caroline cried out, closing her door and wiping at fresh tears. "I can't trust"—she sobbed—"I can't trust John." She meant to say "you" but it was John who was breaking her heart. She plopped onto the chair at her vanity and brought her hands to her face, crying hard. Her heart literally ached.

Spicey set her hand on Caroline's shoulder. "Reverend Mattocks a good man, Miss. He serve people no matter their color. I don't think he can help hisself in so doing. It be somethin' inside him make him do it."

Caroline tried to answer, tried to stop crying. She pulled in deep breaths, tasting her tears, and still, she couldn't stop the pain. Spicey didn't understand the difference this made—didn't realize Papa would never agree to a marriage if he found out. And even if he did agree, then Spicey's position could change. John would surely want to give her freedom as Caroline now realized he'd done with his other slaves.

But she simply couldn't lose him. He was the best thing that had come into her life. "Why did you help him?" Caroline finally managed to say.

"What you mean?" Spicey handed Caroline a corner of her apron.

Caroline wiped at her face with it. "He told me he needed you to show him where a runaway was hiding."

Spicey drew her brows together.

"What are you not telling me, Spicey?"

The girl suddenly started to cry too, wiping at her tears, shaking her head.

"Tell me now, or I'll sell you away. You'll never see me or my family again."

"Please, no Miss!" Spicey fell to her knees and clutched Caroline's hand. "Don't ever sell me." Fear tightened her caramel-colored face, her dark eyes displaying acute pain.

Caroline swallowed her shame knowing she'd caused Spicey's misery, but she needed the truth. "Tell me, Spicey!"

"I not help him. He help me. Annie Mae my friend. She run afore and got on well doin' chores and such for peoples cuz she look white. This time I needed to make sure she not caught again. Her pappy . . . massa . . . wanna make babies with her." Spicey brought her hands together as if in prayer. "Please, Miss. Annie Mae need ta getaway."

Caroline pushed back in her chair, remembering the runaway who looked white—those exotic eyes and filthy dress and hair. "I met her." Annie Mae had told Caroline how desperate she was to stay away from her father. Caroline shuddered. She remembered the desire to help, but all she'd been able to do was give the girl a shawl and bonnet. What good had those things done against a man's unholy desire?

"'Scus'm?"

"I met Annie Mae months ago. Papa and I came upon a bounty hunter who'd caught her." Why hadn't Caroline talked Papa into keeping the girl? All this could've been avoided if Caroline had done so. John would still be hers. Annie Mae would be safe. Spicey wouldn't be keeping secrets.

Bringing her clasped hands to her mouth, Spicey uttered, "Lordy!"

Caroline rubbed her face. "Annie Mae needed to get away—you're right." She looked down at Spicey, who appeared dumb struck. "John helps people, like you said."

"Yessum."

"But what he does is against the law." She took Spicey's hands in hers. "I made him choose between me and his . . . unsavory secret activities."

"You must talk to him. Make this business go away." Spicey stood and began unbraiding Caroline's hair. "He a good man. He'll listen."

"I can't do it. I say all the wrong things. You don't understand how hard it is to be brave."

Spicey's hands stilled. "I unnerstan." She looked at Caroline's reflection in the mirror. "It like bein' in constant prayer, knowin' you cain't do it alone. It's finding courage where you think there's none. I'm just now pluckin' bravery by askin' you to talk to your man." Spicey visibly swallowed. "Cuz if you marry him, he'll take you away from me." A tear slid down her cheek. "Or he'll sail me to Boston for my freedom."

Caroline's hand flew to her chest. "I'll never let anyone take you from me."

"You just say you sell me away."

Caroline pressed her hands against her cheeks in shame. "I didn't mean it. I'd never part with you. I told John that this morning."

"You did?" A smile lit Spicey's face like sunshine had suddenly warmed her. "Ax the reverend to give you another chance. Tell him you can keep his secrets."

Caroline looked deep into the mirror. She looked like the same Caroline she'd always been. The one who ran from confrontation, couldn't stand up to strong feelings of displeasure. When a wrong had been done her, she'd tell herself she didn't care, it wasn't worth the drama of making it right. She'd stayed quiet all her life. It was who she was. "It will sound like I'm begging if I go to John and ask for him to continue courting me. What if he doesn't want me?"

"I see'd the way he looks at'cha," Spicey said. "He want you. You just need to convince him he wants you nuff to make it work—him still doin' what he *need* to be doin' and you supporting him."

ལྟ་ལྟ་ལྟ

As Caroline and Spicey walked to the house John rented, Caroline knew she could no longer be reticent with him. There was too much at stake. She couldn't lose him. She needed to speak her mind and somehow get him back. And what she needed to say, Hester—or any other chaperone—couldn't hear, for John's sake and hers. So, she'd brought Spicey, telling Mama they were going for a walk.

Caroline rubbed vigorously at her cheeks, trying to loosen the dryness her crying had created. She assumed her eyes were still red and swollen, but she didn't want to wait another minute before talking to John.

John answered at her first knock. She was expecting a servant, but of course he didn't have a servant. How foolish she was. Instead, she found John wide eyed, taken aback that she stood before him. "May we come in?" she asked.

"Of course." John opened the door wide and gestured them forward.

"May Spicey stand here in your foyer while we talk someplace alone?"

If she thought John looked surprised to find her at his doorstep, this request caused his mouth to drop open.

He coughed. "By all means." He held up a finger. "Just a moment." He stepped into a room and brought out a chair. "Please sit, Spicey." He gestured to the chair, speaking to Spicey as if she were a lady.

A lady! Caroline had never seen anything more ridiculous.

Taking Caroline by the elbow, he led her into his parlor, leaving the door open.

Caroline stepped to it and closed the door a little harder than she'd meant. It shut with a resounding click. She winced, took a deep breath, and turned to him.

His inquiring but guarded expression reminded her of the proper gentleman he portrayed to others. She needed to get back the John who went out of his way to make sure her needs were met, always caring and comforting her through her troubles. She wasn't going to do it by staring at him and being her old, meek self.

"Shall we sit?" he asked.

"I think I'd rather stand." She took off her bonnet and let it dangle from her hand as she paced to the window and back again. "I can hardly be sympathetic to your cause"—she began, trying to sound resolute—"but in this instance, you were right to help. Annie Mae was in need of escaping evil. How could you have done anything but help?" She stopped her pacing and stood a few feet away from John's side, afraid to look at his face.

"I'm glad you feel that way. I'm not sure your agreement clears up my other . . . activities."

She glanced at him.

His brow furrowed as if he didn't appear to want to negotiate with her.

"If you mean helping other slaves escape, I've been thinking about that too. Is it enough that I know it happens? Can we agree to not talk about it?" She sounded like the old Caroline, the one who avoided distasteful conditions.

John took a slight step away.

She was losing him in this and tried to keep her tears at bay. She couldn't lose John. She knew in her heart they belonged together. Hopefully, someday he'd give up his notions of freeing slaves. In the meantime, she'd need to make sure her family never learned of his activities.

But he remained quiet and she worried he'd already made up his mind.

"You need not give answer now, but I hope you don't leave me wondering for too long." Being forthright was exhausting, and she felt some of her resolve ebbing away. She wanted to slump onto his settee. She couldn't understand how her sisters always kept conversation moving along.

John stepped closer again and took her gloved hand. Surprisingly, he turned it over and kissed her wrist, like he had the first time he came courting.

Some of the tightness in her chest loosened. She touched the back of his head, wishing she hadn't been wearing gloves so she could feel his hair. When he stood, her hand fell to his shoulder. She let it rest there a moment then brought it to his cheek. "Help me know how to keep you."

He smiled, and his dimples weakened her knees. "Being sympathetic to my cause is a start." He tilted his head. "I like this new, determined Caroline."

Just when she thought he'd kiss her, he pulled away. Kept himself in check. He hadn't held her since that time in the church, and she craved to be in his arms.

But her bravery was only going to go so far. She still needed him to respect her. She was raised a lady. She needed to show him she was worthy to be the wife of a preacher.

They went to the door and he showed them out.

CHAPTER EIGHTEEN

Christmas Eve 1859
Harget Plantation, Onslow County

Delighted when Julia shared her plans to have a Christmas party, Caroline spent the week at her sister's plantation home, helping prepare for the event. Society expected Daniel and Julia—as the wealthiest couple in town—to hold elaborate social gatherings. Papa and Mama did not plan to attend. Still in mourning, they felt it wouldn't be proper.

Having lost dear Sarah in October, Caroline had already spent two months in deep mourning and worn only black. Being now in secondary mourning, she could wear purple. She was grateful for a lovely gown of deep eggplant-colored French bombazine sprinkled with cream rosettes on the neckline and across her full-hooped skirt.

"That dress will look right nice with pearls." Spicey moved to Caroline's jewelry satchel. "No need to wear the jet jewels no more." She clasped the necklace on while Caroline attached pearl earbobs to her lobes.

"They 'proprate in secondary mourning cuz they rep'sent tears."

Caroline swallowed down her sadness at the thought of Sarah.

"You look lovely, Miss Carrie." Spicey shifted from one foot to the other. "If you not needin' me no more, all right if I join the other slaves for the party by the cookhouse?"

Since Spicey and John had helped Annie Mae behind Caroline's back, she had a hard time trusting Spicey. Did the girl still keep secrets? "I thought you didn't like mixing with the fieldhands?"

Spicey scrunched her apron in her fists. "I think I want to see what it like. Might be better than sitting up here alone?"

Maybe Caroline's anxiety was over the idea of attending the party, and Spicey wasn't keeping secrets at all. Caroline needed to stop fretting. "Yes, you may attend this once, but I want a full report tonight, you hear?"

"Yessum." Spicey dipped a curtsey.

"Here." Caroline reached into her ribbon box and pulled out a long piece of lace the thickness of ribbon that Julia had given her as a hand-me-down. "Put this around that hair of yours that's always escaping your fabric scraps." She handed the lace to Spicey, who admired it like she thought it a diamond.

Prepared early for the evening, Caroline ambled downstairs to the great hall. Wanting nothing but an enjoyable evening, she turned her attention to the fresh evergreens that draped the front door and stair banisters. Wreaths hung in each window and candelabras were trimmed with ivy leaves and more evergreens.

She peeked into each of the main rooms and discovered greenhouse flowers had been arranged on every table. Deep red poinsettias complimented crisp white orchids and lilies. Oranges shipped in from Florida had been placed on tables in crystal bowls. The house exuded the delightful aromas of citrus, pine, flowers, and spiced cider. The smells of childhood Christmases excited her.

Moments before the guests arrived, a team of slaves lit over a hundred candles, draping the hall and front rooms in radiant light, creating an ambience that Caroline hoped Heaven looked like. *If there was a heaven.*

Although only recently made popular by Queen Victoria, Caroline's favorite decoration was a pine tree atop a large round mahogany table, adorned with small candles, various edibles, and glass trinkets. Julia had acquired the ornaments from Germany where Christmas trees were also fashionable.

The grandfather clock struck six and echoed into the foyer where a few slaves made last-minute preparations.

An hour into the party, both large rooms off the great hall had filled with guests. Cheerful voices and laughter gave Caroline pause to reflect. She felt intimidated by the house full of people, yet loved the silks, velvets, and rich fabrics of all the colorful ball gowns in styles also being worn in European courts. She envied the couples gracefully moving across the dance floor. Why had John not yet arrived? She needed a hand to hold and hoped he wasn't truly unhappy with her. Since their argument about freeing Annie Mae weeks before, they'd found a comfortable peace and gone back to where they'd been before the incident. At least she thought so.

After she'd danced a few times, the musicians took a break. Voices heightened as guests visited. Caroline made small talk with a few cousins.

Surrounded by a dozen people, Julia appeared as a porcelain figure upon a shelf—there to look at, not to touch—obviously the most beautiful woman in the room. Tonight, her cheeks brightened in high color, and Caroline guessed her wicked enough to wear rouge. Married with her own family, Julia wasn't expected to hold to mourning etiquette. At least that's what she'd told Caroline. A festive burgundy velvet dress made Julia stand out. Her large, partially exposed bosom was the only tell-tale sign that she'd given birth to Dolly the month before.

Caroline loved her older sister and used to wish to be like her in both form and charm. But as Caroline became a woman, she hadn't acquired the soft curves Julia had, instead growing tall and slim like their mother. There'd been jealousy on Caroline's part, but it was short-lived because Julia was desperately loyal to all her sisters. And Caroline gave up on the idea that she'd ever have such a vivacious and carefree personality.

She looked about the room for the hundredth time. Where was John? Was she expecting too much? Pushing too hard? They'd only been courting for a month.

"Excuse me, Caroline." A male voice startled her.

Her brother-in-law, Daniel, stood to her right in his own burgundy velvet coat. He was a short but large man with full, brown mutton-chop whiskers rounding his plump jaw. "Would you do us the honor of playing the piano while the musicians take a break?" In one hand Daniel held a drink and in the other an ornately carved silver walking stick.

"Thank you, Daniel," she said quietly, juxtaposing the panic she truly felt. She put a hand to her neck. "But I feel disconcerted . . . in front of all the best of the county. Is there no one else who plays?" Caroline drew herself back, her eyes pleading with his that it be so.

Daniel grinned, apparently unaffected. "Don't be modest," he replied, his voice as thick as sugared dates. "I've heard you play Christmas tunes all week. You play brilliantly. The 'best of the county,' as you say, will be charmed by your talent."

"Is there no one else who plays?" Her chest hitched.

He draped his walking stick over his arm and clasped her upper arm. There was a reason Daniel was the biggest toad in the puddle—he always got his way. Marching her to the piano, he pulled out the stool.

The piano was similar to Caroline's, given to Julia by Papa when she married Daniel. "There's no one else I want to hear, and I'm in need of some festive tunes and singing."

She sat, her billowing purple dress swallowing the round piano stool. Christmas sheet music lay upon the music rack where she'd left it that morning. Leafing through with shaking hands, she passed a new arrangement called "We Three Kings of Orient Are." She'd only that week played it for the first time. That wouldn't do. Thumbing further, she found "It Came Upon the Midnight Clear," a song she'd played many times.

Sitting straighter, she placed her cold fingers above the keys and told herself to remember to breathe. She wished Spicey and John were here to see her bravery. She briefly lowered her eyes and tried to imagine being home with them in her own parlor, then played before her nerves got the best of her. The room quieted and, although she knew the song by heart, she didn't dare look past the notes on the paper.

Daniel's baritone resounded in song, and Caroline breathed easier that some of the attention had been drawn from her. Others quickly joined in, and soon the room filled with spirited chorus. Caroline's fingers fluidly moved over the keys. The nerve-racking experience reformed to exuberance. She smiled inside, relieved that she could finally play in front of people.

At the end of the song, applause broke out throughout the room, and someone called out, "Play another."

"Yes, Caroline, will you?" Daniel moved the sheet music away and found more below it.

Caroline played many more Christmas tunes, becoming lost in the music. The piano her intimate friend, one without expectations, it knew her when she was lonely or afraid and had never let her down. As if music were a living thing, they understood each other.

Although the singing was loud, a peaceful reverence came into Caroline's heart. If this was not the Holy Spirit, she knew not what it could be. Remembering the birth of Christ gave reason to the feeling. This was a season to reflect on her good life and those she loved.

CHAPTER NINETEEN

Fixin to join the group a slaves by the cookhouse, Spicey smoothed her heavy winter skirt and tucked her curls behind the lace ribbon one more time. It not hold her hair any better than her pritty bright scraps. But she liked it much more than them cuz Miss Carrie gave it outta kindness.

Walking toward some black folk, Spicey's stomach chittered like a flock of small birds were inside. The crowd of field slaves and house slaves was larger than she'd ever seen. They were a mix of Harget plantation slaves and the slaves of all the white guests inside. People laughed and greeted each other. Some embraced like it been a mighty long time since they see'd each other last. Not a face looked familiar. She wished Betsey, Cozy or Esther had come, but they in Swansboro mindin' they own duties.

Some men gave her a stare but didn't say nothin'.

She afeared to smile.

Music drifted on the cold air from the open windows of the big house. It not like the nigra music at White Oak Plantation late at night, with fiddling and clapping. This music softer, making her want to glide. Somes doing just that—dancing in the light of torches that smell like pine.

She walked over near 'bout the cookhouse, hoping to catch sight of Junior. Miss said Reverend's brother was comin' to the party, which finally got Spicey brave to ask attendance herself.

Smells of pig roasting made her mouth water, and she wondered if she'd get some or if the white folks eat it all.

"Spicey, dat you?" she heared Junior's drum-beat voice. It pulsed all the way to her bones. Just the sound of it set her heart a thrummin'.

The same feeling from the wagon—heat in her chest—come over her as she turned to find the big man that belonged to the voice. "It me," she said and grinned at Junior, trying hard to act unaffected by her racing heart. Her smile quivered some, and she hoped he couldn't see it in the night gloom. But she could sure feel it.

He stepped close. "Annie Mae jus' fine," he whispered.

And Spicey fancied him all the more for knowing this be her first concern. "Cain't thank you nuff for helpin' her."

He beamed, and she think it the first time she see'd his nice white teeth. There be a large gap in the top center. He a good-looking man.

Another man looking much like Junior, step to his side.

"This Spicey?" the new arrival asked.

Junior elbowed him and scowled, clearing his throat. "Spicey, this be my lame lil brudder, Jerry."

Spicey don't think he little at all, standin' as tall as Junior. "Pleased," she said.

Jerry smiled silly and turned to Junior. "Dat spicy don't lack flavor."

Junior elbowed him a little harder.

"She even mouth-waterin' fiery." Jerry guffawed.

Junior pushed him away, and he laughed louder as he wandered to go visit with others.

Spicey 'spect she should be embarrassed, but people playin' with her name all her life.

More people gather 'round, staring at Spicey like she that pig roasting in the cookhouse. She squirmed some and looked to the ground.

Junior's chuckle sounded uncomfortable when he turn back to her. "These my mam and pappy, Alsey and Jack."

Spicey looked up and smiled shyly, giving a curtsey like she do for Miss Carrie, but then wonder if that 'propriate.

"Hallo there." Junior's pappy take Spicey's hand, and she hoped he didn't notice the tremble.

He patted it between his two hands, real gentle. He not as big as Junior and Jerry, but his wife a tall, straight-backed woman, wearing a turban of clean white cotton.

She scrutinized Spicey some and then said, "Lovely snip a lace in yer hair."

"Thank you, ma'am." Spicey touched the lace.

"Introduce me." Another tall woman pushed Junior outta the way. Her smile as bright as sun sparkling on the White Oak River.

Junior covered his eyes for a moment, then cleared his throat. "Dis my bossy twin sister, Pheriby. She have twins herself. They back home wid her husband."

"Pleasure." Spicey smiled at one of the prettiest women she'd ever see'd, with a long straight nose and heavily lidded eyes. Those black eyes watched Spicey with so much interest, they made her wanna writhe.

"Junior say I bossy, but dat only cuz he cain't work a lick."

Junior threw back his head and laughed when Spicey think he should be riled. "What she not sayin' is dat I spent all day turnin' de soil, and den she ax me ta watch her babies. I done dat while she git all gussied up for dis party, and then she ax me ta bring her some of mam's corn pone, then—"

"Dat nuff, Junior." Pheriby held up her hand. "We all gettin' the meanin'." She tried not to smile, then a giggle broke free. "I guess ya toler'ble," she said to him.

Overcome with so many kin folk in one place, Spicey gaped at em all. How blessed Junior be. Most family members sold off and rare to see a mammy and pappy and chillens all told.

Junior rolled his eyes and stepped away from his kin, taking Spicey's arm. "Y'all can gawk at this pritty gal affer I dance wid her."

Spicey stumbled along. "Junior," she said down low, "I never dance afore."

He stopped and turned to her. "Yer plantation nigras never jig to fireside fiddlers?"

"They do . . . did. I a house slave and never invited."

Junior's brows rise. "So ya never done a field holler either?"

She shrugged, embarrassed. "I sing at funerals is all."

"Well, I'll be!" He stared for a bit. "Let's start by teachin' ya ta dance. Dis music from de big house a white folk, slow song and not a ring shout where we's sing and clap and go in circular motion. I teach ya dat later."

Later? Tonight or another time? Was Junior includin' her in the future?

He put his hand at her waist and showed her to put hers on his shoulder. He took her other hand.

She liked being close to him and keenly aware of where his hands touched her.

With a small smile and gentleness in his eyes, he said, "I step dis way." He stepped to the side. "And you step too." He moved left, and she followed. "We do simple steps tanight."

The music played slow and steady. Junior was a patient teacher, guidin' her about. They danced two more numbers till Spicey felt she had the skill. She growed used to Junior's hands touching her and trusted his movements. She got so comfortable, she stopped counting and could talk to Junior as they danced. He told her 'bout Annie Mae's escape, and she learned that Reverend Mattocks always secretly met him three days affer their parting and brung him home by wagon to Massa Kit's.

Spicey noticed a man dancing with a buxom girl, who watched Spicey and Junior closely. She leaned closer to Junior. "That man"—she jerk her head in his direction—"keep starin' at us."

Junior looked over and laughed, the gap in his teeth a befittin' feature to his charm. "That be my eldest brudder, Joe. He gonna wanna know what we talkin' 'bout."

Spicey pictured the brothers lying on pallets at night, talking 'bout the day's chores or what they think of things—how they feel 'bout certain girls. What Junior say 'bout her tonight?

She saw Junior's mam and pappy dancing together, still looking like they in love. Little smiles and soft words, occasional bursts of laughter.

In Junior, she find integrity. Like Reverend. And she realized how much more important integrity was than what job Junior did in the fields—whether he lived in the big house or in a cabin with a dirt floor. It's not how he talked or the sounds of his words, but what those words meant.

Miss Carrie never thunk such of Spicey. She always thunk herself better. Spicey feel it ain't the truth of things. In the end, they all just bones in the earth. No color of skin remain. Souls in heaven onliest remember peoples' actions and who they were with their deeds. Laws of slavery don't change what in folk's heart.

Junior squeezed her hand. "Have I lost ya?"

She shook her head. "I just thinkin' on my Miss."

"What ya do in de big house?"

"Weave, make cloth, and sew. I also Miss Caroline Gibson's lady's maid and care for her needs. Reverend courtin' Miss Carrie."

"So ya never mix wid de black folk?"

"Oh, I do. There're many house slaves, but work keep me mostly with Miss Carrie or makin' cloth and keepin' her clothes clean and pressed."

"I tole ya in de wagon dat white folk never gonna be yer kin. I'm sorry if what I say hurt ya some."

She nodded, past the hurt of that night. "I just ain't have family other than mayhap a pappy out there somewheres."

"And ya never see'd him afore, I remembra." The dance ended, and they walked toward those milling about a table spread with victuals.

Spicey sighed. "Like you say, he prob'ly not know I exist."

"Important thing is Spicey, ya does exist. And yer a fine person." Junior looked away. Was he embarrassed 'bout his words and how he said 'em with passion? He cleared his throat. "I see'd yer kindness with Annie Mae, and she tole me all ya done for her. We talk 'bout ya till I feels I knowed ya good." He stopped and took Spicey's hand. "You a tender-hearted person who can love and forgive both white folk and black. You come out above all the rest of us." He smiled with closed lips.

She not know what to say. Heat moved up her cheeks when she played his words back in her thoughts. He complimenting her. She remembered the reverend embracing Junior that night of Annie Mae's escape. Mayhap Junior understand Spicey more than she realize. "You git on with Reverend Mattocks?"

"I do. I cain't git slaves outta here wid'out him. And he a good man of God."

"You a good man of God?"

"I have my own sins, I reckon, but I pray, and mam learned me commandments."

Piana music drifted from the open winduhs of the big house. Spicey knowed for a surety it be Miss Carrie playin' the tune. She being brave! The joy of Christmas and the Lord's goodness entered Spicey's soul. And her love for Miss Carrie still there as strong as ever.

Slaves suddenly started singin' the white man's song with a little more rhythm then she ever heared afore. Junior clapped the beat, and the swaying bodies and blending voices gave her a feeling of having come home. Home to the place she'd always been lookin' for.

And ye, beneath life's crushing load,
Whose forms are bending low,
Who toil along the climbing way
With painful steps and slow,
Look now! for glad and golden hours
come swiftly on the wing.
O rest beside the weary road,
And hear the angels sing!

Junior whispered in her ear, "Not long afore we free. I feel it in my soul."

His words seeped into her like water. A thrill of hope moved through her. And for the first time she wanted to be free.

She leaned against Junior, thinking she liked everything about him. He gentle and kind with loving kin who most likely learned him his good traits. "When we see each other again?"

Junior's smile was as comfortable as sitting on a porch swing together, and she think he like her too. "If Reverend Mattocks marry yer miss, mayhap we see each other more offen, for Massa Kit real close to his brudder. I hear 'em talkin' yesterdee 'bout Miss Carrie. She gonna keep his secret 'bout freein' slaves." He cocked his head. "Which remind me . . ." Junior's voice became more serious. "Freein' slaves dangerous business. I sleep bedda if ya leave it ta me."

Spicey bulked at the idea of him telling her what to do, then she realized it cuz he care. "You care? 'Bout me?"

He tucked her arm through his and bring her close, walking with her toward supper. "I do."

Spicey's sure her loneliness could dissolve with the love of Junior and his kin. Mayhap she even have her own family with Junior. The thought filled her with something like when God calm her troubles.

CHAPTER TWENTY

Later that evening, after dancing and watching out for John—who never arrived—Caroline found herself surrounded by guests at the supper table.

The savory smell of roast goose with herb dressing filled the air. Fruits piled high on silver platters, and molded puddings sat on every table.

She marveled at the food. Many slaves must be in the cookhouse to prepare such a feast. Certainly, more than Papa owned.

Sipping fine wine, she looked about. The dining room could scarce seat all the guests. Pressed in tightly, she wouldn't be able to leave until those nearer the doors left first. As she glanced over the merry crowd, she was delighted to finally see John, who was trying to head her way.

He waved and shrugged in resignation, knowing it could take some time to weave around the guests.

She laughed at the absurdity of the situation but felt so very relieved.

"Why do you laugh, Miss Caroline?" John's brother asked. Ned sat beside her. Caroline's sister Mary, Ned's wife, was seated at his other side. His light brown hair curved in slight waves over his ears, as if someone had taken a hot iron to it. Being from a different mother, Ned looked nothing like John. Thinner, his fingers bony and cheekbones sharp, he didn't quite cut the same robust figure.

"Your brother has arrived and can't seem to make his way to us," she said.

"He's been busy preaching the gospel, no doubt," Ned said dryly. "I can't imagine what drives him to live the life he does."

Caroline flinched. The disrespect he had for John stung her. "I'm sure he has good reason to be late." Or did Ned know of John's abolitionist activities and disagree?

Ned wrinkled his nose, his mustache and goatee splayed. He had a somewhat starched personality, and Caroline often found it difficult to warm to him. Occasionally, when she glanced his way, she'd meet his stare. His blue eyes seemed to see all, and he was also often skeptical in his views and spoke in negatives.

She pivoted away from Ned to watch John's progress. Within ten feet of her, someone had stopped him for conversation. He glanced her way, his one-dimpled grin bringing out the love for him she kept trying to contain because she couldn't imagine he felt the same.

Five minutes later, John stood before her. Unlike the formal evening attire of the other men—dark coattails and contrasting trousers with a white cravat tied under pointed collars—he wore his long black clergyman's coat, a high-buttoned cotton shirt, and black trousers.

"Welcome to the party, little brother." Ned stood and grasped John's hand.

John sat in the seat reserved for him, next to her. "Thank you, Ned. Have you been enjoying yourself?"

"Yes. The Hargets surely know how to entertain." With an uncharacteristic wink, he added, "Kit and I did as you asked."

John barely smiled. Ned reclined once again and turned to talk to Mary.

Caroline had watched the brothers' interchange with interest. She didn't quite comprehend their relationship and figured it must be an element of having an older brother. They were always civil, yet Ned often acted as if John was a thorn in his side.

"Please forgive me." John leaned close. "My tardiness couldn't be helped. Old Mrs. Collins passed away this very day, and my services were needed."

The happiness she'd felt at John's arrival instantly diminished, her sympathies with the Collins family. Although she didn't know them personally, she knew well the pain of losing a loved one. "I'm sorry to hear of her passing—and at such a time of year when all should be joyous. How's her family getting by?"

"They're low in spirits but find relief in her escape from suffering. She'd been ill surprisingly long."

"Death is so very final." She'd hoped to have gotten past these sudden moments of sadness and turned away from John.

He took her hand, and she turned back. "I'm sorry to bring sad tidings to such a festive occasion. I've saddened you. Please forgive me. Let's talk of happier topics. Tell me of the party and what I've missed."

Caroline thrilled at his touch and delighted at his thoughtfulness. John was different from any other man she knew. "The musicians are superb. Before our meal, the guests danced for two hours."

"Have you danced?" John asked without looking at her, shifting slightly in his seat.

"Only with your brothers."

John laughed quietly. "I hope you don't mind, but I put them up to it. I figured if they kept you busy, other young men wouldn't fill your time." He smiled his apology. "Do you mind?"

Warm with happiness at his admission, she loved the attention and knowing he felt possessive toward her. "No, I don't mind. I'd much rather dance with you though."

John grinned a smile as fine as the wine. "And that we will do. You have me for the rest of the evening."

An hour later, the candles were half burnt, and the party had a heightened energy. With John's hand on the small of Caroline's back, he guided her through the crowded hall and entered the larger of the two sitting rooms where Negro musicians took seats on a platform in the back.

When John and Caroline found a spot to stand amid the crowd, he removed his hand from her back. She missed his touch instantly.

"Julia and Daniel have outdone themselves. The house is sparkling with Christmas cheer," he said, taking in the elaborate decorations.

Caroline wasn't sure how to take his comment. He'd told her once he thought Christmas was being used as an excuse for parties and drinking. He probably felt it should be a holy day spent at church.

"Do you view the adornments as nonsense?" She watched his face for signs of disappointment.

"Not in the least," he said, smiling at her. "The decorations can make Christmas that much more exceptional. I don't frown upon celebrating the birth of Christ in this manner."

She exhaled with relief. In trying to understand some of his feelings relating to God and theology, she sometimes tip-toed around religious subjects so as not to say or do something wrong. She remembered the reverent feeling she had while playing the Christmas carols. "I find the decorations lovely. My favorite is the tree." She pointed to the table at the side of the room.

"There's a legend that in the seventh century a monk from England went to Germany to teach the Word of God. He did many good works there, and in his teachings of the Holy Trinity, he used a fir tree, which has a triangular shape. The converted people began to revere the fir as God's tree. It eventually became the symbol of Christianity, although many churches dislike a celebration of the birth of Christ."

She wasn't surprised by the short sermon. "Oh, I had no idea—"

"Pardners fo de cotilly-in," a Negro shouted the call to dance.

"Miss Caroline." John favored her with the most formal of bows, bending deeply. He stood straight and reached for her. "Would you do me the honor of this dance?"

"Don't be so formal." Caroline's cheeks heated with embarrassment and pleasure. She glanced around to see if anyone noticed. A few people quickly turned as she caught their eyes. She looked away too. "You make me blush." Wanting to get away from the onlookers, she laughed nervously and took his arm.

He led her to the quadrille, and others filed in, each gentleman with a lady on his arm. The four sets of eight pairs quickly gathered.

The same scrawny Negro who'd called them to dance stepped up on the platform. "Our host and hostess do please open de dance."

Out of the crowd came Daniel with Julia on his arm. A couple stepped away from one of the quadrilles, and Daniel and Julia took the empty place among the waiting couples.

Caroline looked to John, and their gazes locked.

"You look lovely tonight," he whispered.

There was something in his eyes she hadn't seen before. As they joined hands, her pulse raced, her joy in this evening complete to finally be able to dance with him. Even though they were in a room full of people, the ease she often felt when they were alone settled over her.

The sweet notes of the violin filled the room, signaling the promenades to begin, and they stepped into the pattern of the dance, weaving toward and away from one another. Each time their eyes locked, John's expression softened. She thrilled at the interchanges and wondered if John did too.

The pattern soon separated them as they wove around the other dancers. Strains from the stringed instruments heightened Caroline's feelings of bliss. She and John joined again, and he circled her in the figure. As they came together and faced each other, a gleam of passion kindled in his eyes just as she was swept away from him once more.

The controlled carriage of the dancers was poetry in motion. Everyone took turns sweeping gracefully along the length of the quadrille, the women's belled skirts swishing. The slow, deliberate progress brought Caroline again hand in hand with John. His eyes still found only hers. They moved around each other in a complete circle, finished the set, and repeated the dance again. Regrettably, the music soon came to an end, taking away her excuse to touch him publicly.

Off the dance floor, and a bit out of breath, John led her to the edge of the room.

He smiled, and the corners of his eyes crinkled. "I've enjoyed our dance together. Can I bring you some punch or refreshment?"

"No, thank you." Caroline didn't think she could swallow, her throat so tight with emotion. She looked for empty chairs to sit but found none. "If you need some refreshment, I'll wait here."

"I'm fine," he said nonchalantly.

The moment had passed, and John no longer paid her great attention. Instead, he watched the crowd.

Wondering what had changed, she moved closer to him. "John," she said softly, "what were your thoughts while we danced?"

Red crept up his cheeks. With a grin on his face, he briefly glanced at Caroline and then back to the crowd. "What do you mean?"

"Oh, I don't rightly know," she teased lightly. "You appeared as if you had something on your mind. A great secret possibly?" Was he feeling as drawn to her as she to him?

"Perhaps we will talk of it soon," he answered good-heartedly. "I fear I was feeling with my heart and not my head. After all, Christmas is about love." He gave her a glorious, dimpled smile.

Somber-natured, the reverend had been replaced with the John she'd met alone in the church that day. The physical attraction between them couldn't be denied. "I think I want you feeling with your heart more often." She laughed, delighted with this side of him.

"I love it when you laugh," he whispered near her ear.

He gazed at her like he loved more than her laughter, the air between them charged. His eyes dropped to her mouth.

Caroline took a deep, steadying breath as realization burst upon her that she loved John more than anyone she'd ever loved before. She turned away to compose herself. Unwanted tears came to her eyes so quickly she surprised herself as much as John. She knew that controlling her heart at that moment was useless.

"I've a lot to learn about women," he teased. "One moment you're laughing. Then before I take another breath, you have tears in your eyes." Seemingly unaware of anyone watching, he brought her to him with a hand at her waist and with his other hand took hers and brought it to his lips. "Carrie," he whispered, "I care deeply for you."

A shock went through her body, and she yearned to tell him of her love, but such a public display of emotion would be improper. She pulled her hand from his and stepped away, glancing around to see if anyone had seen. She brushed at a stray tear. "We're in a room full of people."

John went still, his back straightened, and he stood taller. In an instant, he was a serious, stuffy preacher. He pulled a handkerchief from his upper coat pocket and handed it to her, his expression pensive. "Can we step out a moment?" he asked in a clipped tone.

She'd obviously upset him when she'd only been trying to protect his reputation, as much as her own by being prudent with her affections. Did he not realize what it was like to be in a relationship with a preacher? Or see the expectations people had? Or understand that she felt as if she could never be good enough. Had he not heard the rumors that some of their acquaintances thought her not fit for John?

Caroline quickly wiped her eyes with the handkerchief, hoping no one noticed their recent indiscretion or her tears.

Before they arrived at the door leading out to the hall, the music stopped and a call went out, "Git yo' pardners fo de Virginny Reel."

People pushed past them, causing a crush toward the dance floor, forcing them to stop. She'd rather follow the rush then deal with her disordered emotions. Once people cleared out of the way, John took her by the arm and led her toward the hall, then out to the back piazza where they were alone.

After being in the stuffy dance hall, the air felt crisp but not unpleasant. A large group of slaves gathered at a distance, outside by the cookhouse, also lining up for the Virginia Reel. The caller's voice and lively music drifted from the house loud enough for the slaves to step in, bow to their partners, and begin to dance. The flickering of torches sent shadows of their dancing bodies across the yard.

Caroline turned to John. The air was cool enough to see his breath. She should've thought to grab her shawl on the way out. At the moment, she still felt overcome with confusing emotions.

"I'm sorry if I made you uncomfortable." He put his hands into his pockets. "I'm unlearned in the ways of courtship."

Tears forgotten, she smiled at his admission. She wanted to tease him, but he seemed too serious for gaiety. He was a grown man who'd traveled halfway around the world, been educated at a university, and taught people Greek and Latin and God's gospel, yet he wasn't sure how to treat a woman. She thought he'd handled it as she would've liked if she hadn't had to fret about tongues wagging.

"I suppose I'm trying to understand what others expect of a preacher and the woman he's courting. You've done nothing wrong. I'm sorry for the tears, but my feelings overwhelmed me. They felt good and right. I think I was surprised and a little embarrassed that the feelings arose in a room filled with so many people."

He made brief glimpses at her face, keeping his hands in his pockets. "You asked me earlier what was on my mind. May I speak honestly of my concerns?"

Concerns? What concerns? Fear stiffened her body. Would he tell her they couldn't be together because of what had happened with Annie Mae? She thought they'd cleared that up. Thoughts of rejection flew through her head. Several excruciating moments passed as she stared at the Negroes dancing and waited for his rejection.

"Carrie?" John took a hand from his pocket and touched her sleeve. His forehead crinkled with a look of concern.

Had she misjudged him? "Please don't tell me you can no longer court me."

"You have my heart, fully and freely. I cannot turn back my feelings of love for you."

Her breath caught. He loved her. But was that enough for him to invite her into his life?

"Lately, I've been considering long and hard what it would mean to be your husband. I'm a selfish man and want you for my own. But I know you well enough to see what that will do to you."

"I don't understand."

He pulled his other hand out of his pocket and grasped both her upper arms, meeting her gaze with an imploring look. "I cannot offer you the life you're accustomed to. A clergyman's salary is nothing compared to your father's income. We wouldn't have the servants you've had all your life." His voice seemed strangled, and he clutched her harder. "How do I dare ask you to cook and clean? What can I offer you? Why would you ever want to leave what you have and come to a life of servitude?" He dropped his head and arms, stepping away. "I'm sorry."

She was still stuck on the word "husband." The rest sounded like nonsense. Yes, she had thought about what it would be like to be a clergyman's wife, but she assumed he'd let her have her slaves after their last talk. Was he saying she couldn't? She quickly dismissed the question and settled on his professions of love. "John, I love you." She swallowed hard. "Walking away because of your income wouldn't be a consideration." She moved closer, wanting to show him he needn't be sad or feel hopeless. And she honestly believed he'd inherit his mother's wealth eventually. Did he not consider that? "I can't lie to you. If we do have a future of poverty, that does scare me, but I can't live without you in my life. It's like you're my solid foundation and life would crumble without you."

John's features relaxed, but his eyes still appeared troubled.

"You think not cooking and cleaning is what brings me happiness? Give more credit to my character." Papa would surely give her slaves as wedding presents for such things.

A battle seemed to be going on behind John's eyes.

The choice was clear. She'd already made it. The question of the slaves could be dealt with later. It should have no bearing on their love.

"Are you *sure* of your feelings?" He gazed at her lips.

"I'm sure." She glanced around to make sure no one stood in the dark corners of the piazza. She wanted not just to tell John she loved him but to show it, yet she couldn't bring herself to touch him. She wanted him to make the first move. She needed to know that he wanted her.

To her relief, he took her in his arms. It was their first embrace since the one in the church. And felt just as wonderful. With no one looking, she let go of her fears, wanting to be free with affection too. She wrapped her arms around him, his body solid and comforting.

He kissed her cheek and finally his warm mouth covered hers.

She eagerly returned his kiss. No matter his worries, she'd make sure to work it out. They belonged together.

The End

Follow the lives and relationships of John and Caroline,
and Spicey and Junior in
White Oak River: A Story of Slavery's Secrets.

www.orasmith.com

White Oak River: A Story of Slavery's Secrets

After giving birth to a son with dominant African traits, a white Southern enslaver must decide if she'll hold onto her bigotry at the cost of her heart.

When Caroline Gibson marries the Reverend John Mattocks, she leaves behind her privileged life, which she finds easier than leaving behind her prejudices. While she's content being served, John lives to serve others. Scorning his family's wealth and long-held practice of owning slaves, he chooses to follow his conscience, becoming an abolitionist preacher. But after Caroline gives birth to a son of African heritage, they both must face their vastly different beliefs. Their marriage mirrors the Civil War's failure to create a changed society, the turmoil not only leaving the nation in despair but their relationship as well. Can their love find deeper roots in forgiveness and acceptance?

This dramatic story of love, faith, family bonds, and discrimination is based on true events of the author's great-great-great-grandparents in coastal North Carolina.

AUTHOR'S HISTORICAL NOTES

In this novella, the names of Reverend John Mattocks, his family members, and Susan "Caroline" Gibson and her family members are true names. The death of ten-year-old Sarah Gibson did happen in October 1859. Her death record is listed in the 1860 Onslow County, North Carolina, Mortality Census, p. 130: "Died at age 10, female, born in North Carolina, died in the month of October of typhoid after being ill for 5 days." Caroline turned nineteen a few weeks after Sarah died.

Caroline was born into an affluent family. Her father William J. Gibson ran a shipping trade where he took barrels of turpentine distilled on his land from longleaf pine, along with barrel staves, planks, and other lumber to the West Indies. There he traded these products of the pine for sugar, molasses, honey, and fruits. The ships then sailed the Gulf Stream currents to the North American cities of Boston, New York, and Philadelphia where the commodities were sold. The 1860 United States Federal Slave Schedule records him enslaving thirty-five human beings. Their names were not recorded.

William Gibson owned a home and estate called White Oak Plantation in the present country area of White Oak near Gibson Branch Creek. His eight-hundred acres spread through both Onslow and Jones Counties. I don't know what happened to the plantation home, but it did survive the Civil War. Caroline lived there until 1890 with her mother. My grandmother had visited there in her youth and my guess is it was demolished in the 1930s. I wish I had asked my grandmother to describe it to me. In 2000, I visited the cemetery off Gibson Branch Road where I believe many Gibsons are buried. Only the headstone of Susan Simmons

Gibson, Caroline's mother, remains partially above ground with dozens of unmarked graves surrounding her, the depressions in the earth approximately seven feet by three feet in shape. There are photographs of the town home in Swansboro, called Gibson House, and it looked as I described in this story. It stood at 302 Main Street on the northeast corner of Main and Elm Streets and was demolished in the 1970s. A bank was eventually built at that location, then another. But before the second bank was built, I was able to visit the cleared land and look down the green sloping hill to the White Oak River. Although there are now buildings on the hill and Highway 24 cuts across its slope, I could imagine it without those obstructions and with one of William's ships alongside the Gibson pier.

Across from the bank on Main Street, still standing is the Ringware House (circa 1778 and on the National Register of Historical Places). Possibly the oldest house in Swansboro, this is where Daniel and Julia Harget (now spelled Hargett) once lived. There are stories of the Ringware House being haunted and piano music sometimes heard. Daniel Harget was one of the wealthiest gentlemen in Onslow County and owned a country plantation where the scene of the Christmas party is set. His descendants have no records of the house's size or exact placement because it was burned by the Yankee's during the Civil War. Julia Gibson Harget was truly a beauty, but her personality traits are conjecture in this story.

The name of Spicey is fictitious, but Caroline would certainly have had a personal lady's maid. The names of Annie Mae, Betsey, Cozy, Zylphia, Moses, Big George, Joe, Ezra, Hanna, Jess, and Esther are also fictitious as are the enslaved of Christopher "Kit" Mattocks. Although in the 1880 United States Federal Census, well after the War, a black servant is recorded in the household of Kit Mattocks with the name of "Alsey," age 66. Twenty years before, Kit enslaved six people according to the 1860 United States Slave Schedule: a 50-year-old male, 45-year-old female (Alsey?), 25-year-old male, 21-year-old female, 21-year-old male, and an 18-year-old male, thus I created Junior's family. Kit was a physician, as was his stepfather Philip Koonce. These family connections and occupations become more important in the novel *White Oak River*.

It is true that runaway slaves hid in the Croatan Forest (now a national forest containing 160,000 acres and named after the Indian tribe living in the region at the time of the 1587 Lost Colony). Those slaves could have seen and experienced everything from thousand-year-old cypress trees, bogs, saltwater estuaries, deer, black bears, turkeys, insect-eating plants, peregrine falcons, poisonous reptiles, alligators, hundreds of varieties of fish, and moonshiners working their stills. A runaway slave route of the area was to board a ship along the Neuse River, where a known network of sympathetic watermen assisted those desiring freedom. How many slaves followed this route is unknown, nor do any detailed stories exist that I could find.

William Gibson did give all his daughters pianos on their wedding days or birthdays. The square grand piano once belonging to Caroline Gibson Mattocks is still in my family. My great-grandmother used to say her husband (Caroline's grandson) would part with her before he'd part with the piano. William bought the five pianos on a trip to Boston possibly in 1851. The date is stamped on my family's piano, which also includes the maker's name and location—Hallet and Davis, Boston. The piano has ornately carved barrel legs and looks as I described. I am not a pianist but have tickled its ivories. Someone in every generation has played the piano while family and friends gathered around it to sing. To my and my grandmother's enjoyment, my son played us the *Star Wars* theme, the tones a brighter timbre than a modern piano, and about one octave short of a regulation keyboard. I have also seen Julia's piano and a third piano believed to have belonged to Mary. They are similar in that they are each square grands but not exactly the same in style or maker. While I can't confirm it, I've been told the one belonging to Hester was hidden in a swamp to keep the strings from the Yankees during the Civil War invasion of Swansboro. It was said the Union troops wanted the strings to make cannons shoot a greater distance. This doesn't make a lot of sense to me, but perhaps there was some other reason?

In 1859, John Mattocks lived on Elm Street in the rented or "borrowed" home of Abe Watson while Abe was in Florida. In a New Bern newspaper dated 29 May 1860, a story is recorded of John Wilkins "a supposed free negro" coming to John Mattocks's home late one night asking for John to sign a document stating that Wilkins was not Negro and could marry a white woman. John signed the paper, creating some unsettling feelings in others. I have no proof that John helped runaway slaves, only records showing he welcomed African Americans into his church after the Civil War ended, when they were allowed by law to attend. In *The Christian Advocate* newspaper, John's one-sentence obituary is a scant bit of detail, and I believe a slap in the face from those who didn't like him. Other ministers were given half a page or more of tribute upon their deaths. In the same newspaper, on the same page as John's obituary, his aunt's obituary is long and filled with overblown prose. She was proslavery and did much to help the Confederacy.

My third great-grandparents, Reverend John Frederick Mattocks and Susan "Caroline" Gibson did marry. In fact, I'm named after their oldest daughter, Ora, but that's all I'm going to say on that subject. Read *White Oak River* to learn more of their story. Regarding John's early life, I found his 1856 Passport Application, but whether he went to Israel or not, I do not know. I have a list of many of the highly academic books he owned. Among them are works related to the history of the Jews, so I assumed he must have had an interest. He attended Trinity, which became Duke University. He taught youth the subjects of Latin and Greek at Swansboro Male and Female Academy, and it appears he had a rapport with the youth. He served as both a local minister and circuit rider as early as 1858. I possess his pocket Bible and large family Bible, in which he wrote on a front page, "This book is never to leave my family. Swansboro, NC 1860," with his signature penned. We have honored his wish.

An ingénue, Caroline is naïve and intolerant in this novella, but the effects of adversity and the Civil War teach her hard lessons many were forced to learn in her day. She became someone I wish I could have known in life. Continue reading her story in *White Oak River: A Story of Slavery's Secrets*.

To see maps, a family group record, and real photographs of many of the characters in this novella, see the novel *White Oak River: A Story of Slavery's Secrets* or visit www.orasmith.com

ACKNOWLEDGEMENTS

This novella was once part of the novel *White Oak River*, but when the novel became too long, I broke the book into two stories and created *White Oak Plantation*. I had written many scenes through Spicey's point of view and played with the idea of her having her own book. But then I realized it may be better for the reader to experience the point of view of a slave owner and the point of view of the enslaved for a comparison of sorts. With that said, some of those who helped me with Caroline's point of view scenes never read Spicey's, and they may be surprised to see their names here below. Yet I do remember their kindnesses to me, so I wanted to thank them both here and in the Acknowledgements of the novel.

My deepest thanks to Vickie Mattocks, a partner in research and a friend. It was fun to share ideas and find records with someone who loved genealogy too. Who else would want to sit side by side in an archive and be thrilled at finding a loose estate paper, half torn and hard to read?

Frances Henderson, thank you for taking in a fellow researcher but stranger and being my first friend and hostess in Swansboro. Thank you for editing and teaching me the lesson on Split Infinitives. You are a patient lady! I will treasure my memories of cemetery hunting with you and you showing me the broken and leaning headstone of Reverend John F. Mattocks so I could fix it before it was lost to history.

Mel Guss, much thanks for helping me discover the Gibson cemetery in the woods on a cold November day in 2000, consisting of rows and rows of seven-foot by three-foot indentations in the ground, with the one remaining visible headstone of Susan Simmons Gibson ("Mama"). I will always remember your kind helplessness when you stood by and watched me cry over her grave. (Mel's wife is a descendant of Julia and Daniel Harget. She and Mel live on the land where the plantation used to stand.)

Thank you, Mary Fulford Moore, for giving me a place to stay and being a great friend when I came to North Carolina to do research. You love discovering family as much as I. Maybe someday I will write the story of our earliest ancestors who disembarked at an unsettled Chesapeake Bay area? Thank you for reading the first version of this story.

I appreciate the kindness of Roger Kammerer who let me and fellow researchers go through boxes and boxes of genealogical documents in his shed. You graciously gave me permission to use in the novel a sketch of Reverend John Mattocks, drawn when a teenager from a photograph. I was never able to find the original photograph, and I'm hoping someone who reads this novella may know where it is located.

Thank you for the advice from my writing groups: The PP Ladies—Cindy Higginson, Sandra Scott, Evelyn Nelson, Anne Law, Lecia Crider, Jan McBride, Luann Roberts, and Kathy Olson. American Night Writers Association chapters of Salt River Scribes, Daytimers, The Write Stuff, and Time Spinners. And the small writing groups that branched off writing classes—Patti Hulet, Juliet Peterson, Margaret Turley, Anna Arnett, and Louise Laughlin. Your encouragement and suggestions made all the difference.

Thank you Pamela Goodfellow for being my first creative writing teacher. You believed I could do it, and that's what I needed to hear.

Dean Hughes, thank you for taking time to read a rough first draft of this story and giving a newbie direction. Your desire to help others write well is admirable, and I am grateful to be a recipient of your kindness.

Thank you to the many who helped with research and writing craft: Alex McGilvery, Steve Shaffer, Dennis Jones, Wayne Venters, and Ethlyn Sanders Hurst. Special thanks to Julia Harget Stephen's granddaughter Lottie Venters Kesler, who lived to be one hundred years old and gave me a tour of her Antebellum home. It was there that I saw Julia's square grand piano given to her by William Gibson.

Thank you to my original 2014/2015 beta readers, who read a formidably long version of this story when it was called *Choices*. You all gave me helpful advice—Janette Penfield Rasmussen, Patti Hulet, Cindy Higginson, Sandra Scott, Mary Hydrick, Jill Hydrick, Amy Lake, Kamela A. Watson, William Reed, Catherine LaPorte, Carter Hydrick (who suggested the title of the novel be *White Oak River*), Christi Hydrick, Rick Hydrick and Jordan Smith.

Feedback from beta readers is always helpful and I appreciate the time they took with my novella. Thank you, Susan Nelson, Patti Hulet, Sandra Sorenson-Kindt, Beth Sexton, Carter Hydrick, and Linda Leigh Hargrove.

Lori Freeland is my fantastic editor, whose keen insight with not only how a sentence can read better but how to bring more meaning into certain scenes, is so very much appreciated. Thank you for your patience, talent, and wisdom.

I will forever be thanking Rene Allen and Jo Ellen Guthrie for the many hours we read our scenes together. You two have heard every book I've written and gave thoughtful and constructive advice. The friendships we developed were the best payoff.

And thank you especially to my Heavenly Father and the inspiration that comes through Him.

ALSO BY ORA SMITH

Children's Picture Book

A Christmas Story of Light

Heritage Fiction

The Pulse of His Soul: The Story of John Lothropp, a Forgotten Forefather

The Cry of Her Heart
a companion novella to *The Pulse of His Soul*

White Oak River: A Story of Slavery's Secrets
the continuing story of *White Oak Plantation*

Unacknowledged
(to be released fall 2021)

Ora Smith, a genealogist who writes Heritage Fiction, creates fascinating stories about her ancestors based on true events. She loves nothing better than to be whisked off to past eras to meet those whose lives are worth sharing.

The Pulse of His Soul: The Story of John Lothropp, a Forgotten Forefather

Based on a true story of love and loss, family and faith.

At the height of Separatist suppression and enforced Anglican worship in England, Reverend John Lothropp meets and marries Hannah Howse. The witty, educated vicar's daughter immediately challenges his decision to put God before a wife. In a world spiraling into hypocrisy, tyranny, and betrayal, Hannah refuses to break from her Anglican roots. But when John comes face-to-face with his deep-seated convictions about religious freedom, he's forced to make a hard choice—renounce his orders with the Church of England to become an outlawed Separatist or conform and save his marriage, his family, and his life.

Considered one of the most important ministers to follow in the footsteps of the Plymouth Pilgrims, John Lothropp helped plant the seeds of religious freedom in America's soil and left a legacy of well-known individuals who influenced the nation's destiny.

The Cry of Her Heart

A companion novella to *The Pulse of His Soul*

Punished for her choice to leave the Church of England and meet illegally with the secret Separatist community, genteel Penninah Howse is thrown into Clink Prison with little chance of release. To survive prison under the evil of Bishop William Laud's tyranny, she must evade the advances of a malicious jailer, learn to live with a cruel cellmate, and battle the enemies of hunger, filth, vermin, and self-doubt. When Robert Linnell finally succeeds in buying visitation rights, her old and dear friend not only brings food, he brings hope. Is there a chance he'll find a way to secure her release? Or will this be her life forever?

Watch for another **Heritage Fiction** about Ora Smith's ancestors in *Unacknowledged* to be released fall 2021.

Unacknowledged

A mysterious letter written on a deathbed. A Texas prostitute who became the mistress of a famous and wealthy entrepreneur. A son born out of wedlock who may have grown up to be a notorious American celebrity. Those vowed to secrecy have died, but the world's curiosity is still very much alive. Don't miss *Unacknowledged*, Ora Smith's third historical fiction novel based on the fascinating lives of her ancestors.

Get free novellas, sign up for Ora's newsletter, and get to know Ora at www.orasmith.com

amazon.com/author/orasmith
bookbub.com/authors/ora-smith
facebook.com/AuthorOraSmith
instagram.com/authororasmith
twitter.com/AuthorOraSmith

ABOUT ORA SMITH

Ora is an artist, genealogist, seamstress, lover of a good book, traveler, antiquer, upcycler, and history buff. She's one of those people who always has a project she's excited about. Although she's lived in Arizona since 1986, she spent her early life in Lake Tahoe, California, where her passion to write blossomed on a tranquil riverbank with a beautiful backdrop of the Sierra Nevada Mountains.

Made in United States
Orlando, FL
18 November 2024